A single wrong step could mean their end.

THE DANCER AND THE DARK

Gavin Wallace has a problem, and her name is Chloe Reardon.

For years, Gavin and Chloe have built a life together, skirting the vampire world as much as possible. Chloe has continued dancing, and Gavin has continued building a business empire.

But for a vampire in love with a mortal, nothing about the future is certain.

When an unexpected loss compels Chloe's return to her childhood home, she's forced to face the reality of her mortality and decide what her future will hold.

Will she turn toward humanity or follow her lover into the dark?

The Dancer and the Dark is a novella set in the Elemental universe and the second in Gavin and Chloe's story by *USA Today* best-selling author, Elizabeth Hunter.

D1591206

THE DANCER AND THE DARK

A DEVIL AND THE DANCER NOVELLA

ELIZABETH HUNTER

The Dancer and the Dark
Copyright © 2022
Elizabeth Hunter
ISBN: 978-1-941674-95-6
Paperback edition.

Cover: Damonza
Content Editor: Amy Cissell
Line Editor: Anne Victory
Proofreader: Linda, Victory Editing

Recurve Press LLC
PO Box 4034
Visalia, California
USA

1

Gavin Wallace sat across from the two vampires glaring at each other from either side of the elaborate Russian tea service he'd ordered. He poured the fragrant tea into a delicate blue-and-white cup.

"Tatyana," he said, "how much sugar would you like in your tea?"

"No sugar," she said. "A spoon of honey only please."

"I take my tea black," Oleg said.

"He didn't ask," Tatyana said.

"Neither did you," the gruff Russian answered. "And yet your caravan encroaches on my territory."

Gavin swallowed the sigh that wanted to release. So they *weren't* making room for polite conversation. At least that would save time. He'd come to his tearoom in Paris for this meeting, and when it was settled, he could return to the States.

Tatyana bit out something in Russian and Oleg started to reply, but Gavin interrupted them both.

"Cake?" He held a plate of petit fours in the center of the table. "I cannot tell you how delighted I am with the new pastry chef here. You both must try them and tell me what you think."

Tatyana didn't move her eyes from Oleg's, but she reached out, took a delicate pink cake, and bit into it, baring two long, slightly curved fangs as she tasted the pastry. "Exquisite."

Gavin didn't react when the two immortals began to argue; neither did any of the silent servers near the doors.

His businesses were known for being discreet and neutral. Gavin never had a problem starting a new property in a city because vampires in charge of large cities where immortals might clash appreciated an impartial meeting place where they could be assured of safety.

Gavin took the opportunity of a pause in the arguing to gently intervene. "If I may...?"

The glaring subsided slightly, and both vampires bit their tongues.

"Excellent." This was, after all, the reason Oleg had negotiated this meeting via his manager in Paris; it wasn't solely because Tatyana was in Paris for a wine-marketing convention. They had a border dispute hanging between them, and it threatened to upend both vampires' businesses.

Gavin cajoled and maneuvered the conversation until both combatants were forced to acknowledge the other's perspective. He revealed nothing of his own thoughts on the matter. His own thoughts were immaterial. And two hours later, he leaned back as business secretaries and contract writers were introduced and terms began to take shape.

In the end, Tatyana and Oleg's confrontation would be settled with gold instead of lives, a preferable outcome for all. This was why Gavin was so careful to cultivate a neutral position. Conflict was hammered out over tea and cake, not blood and iron.

Did Gavin play host to some truly horrendous people? Undoubtedly. But he never let his disdain be known, and he treated everyone as a guest.

His mentor had offered him a proverb when he'd started his first vampire club, and he'd never forgotten it: never back a cat into a corner.

Every immortal needed an off-ramp, especially the most hot-tempered. Every conflict needed a release valve. Unless there was a place to talk, every immortal dispute would end in violence.

Fortunately, this one ended with dessert.

"So your meeting went well?"

He smiled just at the sound of her voice. "It did."

"Are you bringing me some of Michel's petit fours?" Chloe Reardon, his human lover of nearly five years, yawned over the phone. "You better be."

Gavin glanced at the small refrigerator in the plane he had boarded in Paris. "Of course I am. They're not going to be fresh though. Michel wasn't pleased when I told him it would be a few days before I saw you. He was protesting that you needed to come taste them in Paris."

"Obviously I need to do that." She groaned a little.

Gavin detected an undercurrent of pain. "Is your knee hurting again?"

"I'm just a dancer turning thirty this year, O kilted one. Nothing to worry about."

Well, that was impossible.

"Do you need to see a physician? Would a steroid shot

help?" Prior to meeting Chloe, Gavin had little knowledge of the dancing world. After meeting her, he had the utmost admiration. Chloe, in addition to being a phenomenal artist, was also an athlete in constantly peak condition. She had no downtime and no off-season. The wear on her joints was brutal.

"I promise I'm fine." She yawned again. "As soon as this show is over, we should go to Paris."

"Now that we have the plane, it's a matter of a few hours." As a wind vampire, Gavin's nature had rebelled against a private plane for years until Veronica, his longtime assistant, mentioned that it was far more secure for her and his other human staff and security to fly privately.

And sadly, not even Gavin's immortal speed could match the five to six hundred miles an hour that the converted cargo jet could fly.

Eventually he gave in and started a shared charter company with other immortal clients. Within a year, it was turning a handsome profit.

Owning anything in partnership felt like being tied down—something he'd resisted for over 150 years—but times changed, people changed, and the world turned.

He looked around the near-empty passenger cabin. "It feels strange flying with only Veronica and Semis with me."

"Oh, how did Semis like Paris?"

"He liked it, but he had to duck under a lot of doors."

"Oh yeah. I can see that being a problem for him in Asia too."

"He's accustomed to it there."

Gavin's new day man was a massive Samoan footballer he'd met when he renovated his club in Hong Kong.

Semis had been working his way up through the security arm of Gavin's organization and had requested a move to New York the year before to be closer to his sister at NYU.

Chloe was the one who picked him to guard Gavin personally. He trusted her read on the quiet man, and he hadn't been disappointed.

Gavin felt dawn beginning to tug at him, so he secured himself into a small chamber at the rear of the plane.

It wasn't unheard of for vampires to own modern aircraft, though because of their amnis—the electrical current that ran beneath their skin and connected them to their elements—the planes had to be specially fitted with nonconductive insulation.

Modern electronics and vampires didn't get along. Most of his peers were attracted to classic technology and transportation for more than aesthetic reasons.

He was currently using an old traditionally wired phone with a speaker attachment that ran through the pilot's cabin. It was like something fitted into planes in the 1980s, but Gavin didn't care. Most of the vampire world had converted to Nocht, a vampire-friendly software owned by Patrick Murphy, the vampire lord of Dublin, but Gavin had issues with Nocht.

As in privacy issues.

He was paranoid and he wasn't shy about it. This current trip to see his mentor in New Orleans, long over-due, was partly for personal reasons but mostly about business. There was an opening for a Nocht competitor, and he was going to get his mentor to back him in the project.

Marie-Hélène did love upsetting the apple cart.

He heard Chloe yawn again. "You should go to sleep. I'll call you when I land."

"When will you get to New Orleans?"

"At four in the afternoon local time," Gavin said, "so Semis and I will be waiting in the hangar until after nightfall. Veronica will start briefing Marie-Hélène's people as soon as we land."

"Okay." She sighed. "I miss you."

"I miss you too." He missed her like mad, but she had a life, and it wasn't following him around to business meetings. She had friends and work in New York. She danced in the space between the vibrant theater community and the dark vampire collective. For now it was a balancing act she gracefully walked.

For now.

Gavin knew that eventually Chloe would have to make a decision. And for him, the thought of her following a human life grew more and more fraught with dread.

He loved her. He hadn't loved a being more than her in over 150 years. To him, she *was* eternity.

And Gavin had no idea what he'd do if she didn't choose him.

2

_____

Chloe woke a little before noon and her knee was already hurting. She lay in bed, slowly going through gentle stretches to loosen the joint as her cat wound around her, yowling and trying to force her to the food bowl.

"Stop it, drama king." She nudged the black shorthair away and sat up in the massive king-sized bed in her room. The windows were shaded, but she could see midday light pouring through them.

Chloe leaned against the headboard and closed her eyes, still moving her knee in gentle motions. She reached for the phone on her bedside table and tapped a few buttons to put on her morning playlist. Immediately Nina Simone poured through the speakers in her room.

She drank from the bottle of water on her bedside and mentally ran through her day. She was due at Ben and Tenzin's place at one, work for about five hours, then back home for a light dinner before she headed to the theater for the show.

She was performing at Lincoln Center with the

dance company she'd joined on a semiregular basis two years before. She wasn't the star of the company, but she was a regular member for the season and she was loving it. The show at Lincoln Center would run for three more performances, and then they'd have a monthlong break.

While some of her fellow dancers were doing passion projects on their hiatus, Chloe was taking it easy and giving her body a rest.

She got out of bed, her knee barely a twinge, and walked to the luxurious bathroom Gavin had surprised her with the year before. She'd been out of the country with Ben and Tenzin, so he'd had her bathroom remodeled and it was glorious.

That was, it was glorious until she flipped on the lights and saw her reflection in the mirror.

Leaning forward, she blinked her puffy eyes. "Stop talking with your vampire boyfriend until three in the morning, Chloe."

She kept her bonnet on as she warmed up the water to wash her face. Her skin felt dry, so she smoothed some lotion over her body, then rinsed her face, pressing the warm washcloth to her swollen eyes.

It wasn't just the late nights—she was used to those— it was spring in New York and her allergies were going overtime. Gavin had put air purifiers all over the house, had the filters changed to HEPA certified, and made the penthouse as hypoallergenic as possible, but there was only so much a wind vampire could control.

Pollen happened.

Allergies only emphasized the fine lines that were growing around her eyes. She leaned closer, examining them.

"You're turning thirty," she told her exhausted reflection.

And by all human metrics, her skin looked amazing, even during allergy season. She'd never suffered much from acne or other teenage skin conditions. Her mother still looked like she was in her late forties or early fifties, though she was pushing seventy, and as much as she disliked the woman who'd given birth to her, Chloe had to admit she looked like her twin.

But Chloe wasn't comparing herself to humans—she was comparing herself to immortal beings who didn't age.

You're turning thirty.

And she still looked far younger than Gavin, whose human life had been much harder than hers. He didn't talk much about it, but people in the 1870s just aged differently than your average twenty-first-century American.

Her phone started buzzing at her while she had a mask on her face. She tapped the button and put it on speaker. "Hello, Audra."

"Morning. Any changes in the schedule from yesterday?"

Audra was her personal security guard, and Chloe was grateful for her. While she'd struggled at first to understand who would want to harm a very nonthreatening human, she understood that to Gavin's rivals, she was considered a weakness. He'd made it clear that leaving her unguarded was leaving himself open to manipulation.

Chloe was determined that no one would use her to get to Gavin, so Audra stayed.

She dunked a washcloth in the warm water. "Same schedule as last night. Gavin's home tomorrow evening?"

"That's the plan unless his meeting with MHC veers off track."

Chloe smiled. She'd never met Gavin's mentor, Marie-Hélène, but most of his employees who knew her spoke of the eccentric vampire from New Orleans with obvious affection. Gavin and Chloe kept making plans to go down to New Orleans so Chloe could meet the woman, but something always seemed to interrupt them.

"We really need to get down to New Orleans for a trip," Chloe mused. "We keep saying that."

"We do, and something always comes up," Audra said. "Usually involving your employers."

"I'm assuming you don't mean Phillip."

"Your dance director isn't nearly as unpredictable as Ben and Tenzin."

Chloe smiled and wiped the mask off her face, revealing glowing brown skin. She dotted on some serum and patted it in. "I know they're problem children, but I love them anyway."

Only Chloe could get away with calling two of the most powerful vampires in the world "problem children." But she'd known Ben when he was human, and Tenzin? Well, Chloe was the only one who knew the ancient vampire's internet browsing history, and she'd use it for leverage if she needed.

"Audra, I'll meet you down in the lobby in about an hour, okay?"

"Sounds good."

The music clipped on again, and Chloe smoothed face cream over the planes of her cheeks, her chin, and her forehead, gently tapping it on the delicate skin around her eyes.

You're turning thirty.

And her life was good. Her life worked. She loved her life. She loved her boyfriend, and she loved her friends and her work and the crazy city she lived in.

It was good. It was all good.

The music switched, and "I Think It's Going to Rain Today" started.

Chloe tapped forward on her phone and jumped to the next song.

"Tenzin, where did you put the building plans for the job in Mumbai?"

Chloe was furiously looking through the map drawer in Ben and Tenzin's two-story loft, but she couldn't find them. She'd even checked in the file room downstairs she'd manage to wrangle into organizational submission a few months before.

Nothing. The plans were gone.

Tenzin, the ridiculously old wind vampire who paid Chloe's bills, flew out from the loft where she spent her waking hours during the day. It was fully shaded from any of the sun's rays and allowed her quiet and space where she meditated if she wasn't working.

She hovered twelve feet over the ground, just above the french doors that led out to the roof garden. "I put them in the map drawer."

Chloe looked up. "They're not here."

"Then Ben moved them."

Chloe sighed. If Ben had moved them, that meant she wouldn't find them until nightfall. Her old friend had to sleep during the day, unlike his mate.

"Are you sure you put them back?"

Tenzin frowned. "No."

She bit her tongue. "So... you might have put them someplace else?"

"Yes." Tenzin's eyes drifted. "I was looking at the elevator shafts..."

Chloe nodded. "I remember you talking about using them for entry."

"And I..." Tenzin rolled slowly in the air, thinking. "I took them to the roof because the museum was built during the same era as this building, so I was wondering what the access would look like for the elevator shaft, but..." She pointed at Chloe. "Then I remembered that the elevators in Mumbai were later additions to the existing palace structure, so they would be more modern than our building, so I flew down to find out which architects had designed the remodel, but then Ben and I got into an argument about the relative benefits—if you could call them benefits—of French versus British colonial structure in Asia, and I told him—"

"The architectural plans are still on the roof, aren't they?"

Tenzin pointed at her. "Probably."

Chloe sighed. Hopefully the plans Ben had managed to buy from a contact in Mumbai hadn't been blown off the roof and weren't sitting somewhere on Fifth Avenue or drifting in the Hudson. "Okay, from now on, when you need to check something, maybe just make a copy and don't take the originals."

Tenzin frowned. "How do I make a copy of the big plans?"

Dammit, that was a fair question. "Okay, maybe we just keep all the big plans like architectural or building schematics *on* the map table from now on. Or in the map drawer." She spread her hands. "What do you think?"

"Obviously we should," Tenzin said. "Some of those plans are very hard to find. And very expensive to acquire illegally."

Like the Mumbai plans. Chloe clasped her hands together. "Exactly."

Tenzin sighed. "I sure hope the plans on the roof are still there. Ben needed them."

It was a fifty-fifty chance Tenzin even remembered she'd been the one to take them up there. Chloe closed her eyes and made a mental note to ask Ben to retrieve them when he woke.

At first Tenzin's absentminded nature had confused Chloe. The ancient wind vampire was one of the most feared creatures in the immortal world. She was a brilliant tactician and could draw plans of a ninth-century Han settlement from memory or translate a document from Sanskrit to Mandarin with ease. She knew her way around ancient and modern cities, could plan a full-blown military campaign with five hours' notice, and also knew how to knit.

A few months after Chloe had begun working as Tenzin's day assistant, she'd realized something: Tenzin's brain was full.

Five thousand years of information had simply left no room for trivial things like relocated maps, her email password, or which dry cleaner was holding Ben's favorite coat.

So in addition to online research, day errands, and meeting humans, Chloe's duties expanded to acting as Tenzin's peripheral brain.

She glanced at the next thing on her list. "Okay, have

you replied to your father yet? He's invited both you and Ben to a birthday celebration for..." Chloe looked at her notes. "Erden?"

Tenzin's head swung toward her. "Erden? I didn't know Erden was still alive."

"He's hanging in there. Turning one hundred, and there's supposed to be a party in Penglai."

"When? We should go to that. I believe he's my father's oldest human servant."

"It's a few weeks before Christmas here, and I know Giovanni and Beatrice said they'd be in LA this year instead of Rome, so I'm assuming Ben will want to—"

"Ben will want to be with Sadia, but we should have enough time to go to the party too." Tenzin sighed. "I'll write my father. Can you arrange a messenger for tomorrow night?"

"I can." There were couriers whose only job was to safely transmit formal correspondence for vampire clients; Chloe had several in her address book. She looked at the next point on her list. "Gavin is home tomorrow night, so you remember I'm taking the night off, right?"

"Where is he coming from?"

"Uh..." Chloe checked that off. She wasn't going to remind Tenzin a dozen times; if she forgot, Ben would remind her. At least Ben's brain wasn't full. "New Orleans. He's in New Orleans tonight, meeting with Marie-Hélène."

Tenzin narrowed her eyes. "Marie-Hélène?"

"Yes, she and Gavin are doing... a thing. I don't actually know, but there's some kind of joint business thing he wanted to talk to her about."

"Interesting."

Chloe wondered if Tenzin knew any more about

Marie-Hélène's business than Audra did. Sometimes she thought Audra kept a closed mouth because she didn't know how much Gavin wanted Chloe to know.

Irritating? A little, but Chloe guessed it was fair. Audra was security, not Chloe's informant.

"What does Marie-Hélène do?" Chloe asked Tenzin. "I know Gavin refers to her as his mentor. Does she own clubs?"

Tenzin cocked her head. "Of a sort."

Chloe knew there were some vampires who kept nothing but glorified human farms where vampires could drink their fill, but she didn't think Gavin would consider a person who ran a club like that his mentor.

"A sort of... social club?"

Tenzin brightened. "That's an excellent way to classify them. When Marie-Hélène was human, she was the most successful madam in New Orleans. Her brothels were legendary."

Chloe blinked. "Okay. Well, I guess you could classify a brothel as a social club."

"And very egalitarian too. She took women and men of all races and ages. I never went to one, but I heard about them. They were not typical brothels."

"I have no idea what a typical brothel would be, so—"

"Oh, there is a great variety of brothels." Tenzin was obviously interested in the subject. "As I'm sure you know, sex work is one of the oldest professions in the world."

"You are old enough to know."

"Exactly." Tenzin perched on the edge of her loft. "She started out with typical brothels as a human, but as she made more money, she wanted to distinguish herself and her clubs."

Chloe smiled. "Gotta have an angle, right?"

"As there was no lack of brothels in New Orleans, you are correct. Marie-Hélène was educated—self-educated, I mean. She was an avid book collector and had read about geisha culture in Japan. She was determined to create an American equivalent in what she considered the most cultured city in the Americas."

"New Orleans, of course."

"Of course." Tenzin waved a careless hand. "What was New York at the time? Nothing but banks according to Marie-Hélène. She had sex workers upstairs in her clubs, but that was for an extra fee. Social-club members could visit her houses for more chaste entertainment. Her employees were trained singers and dancers, musicians of all kinds. Trained conversationalists who were educated and informed about business and current events. She always had a few who could speak different languages for visiting dignitaries, and artists of all kinds. Painters especially. Sometimes poets would stay there just so they could write poetry about her regulars."

Chloe smiled. "That's kind of brilliant."

"Very brilliant. Not only did she make far more money than her competitors, she counted many prominent people as friends. And since her clubs were classified as social clubs, their friendship could be public. She was considered an art patron, not a sex broker."

Chloe could definitely see why Marie-Hélène had attracted immortal attention. "And after she became a vampire?"

"Not much changed except she and her sire started numerous other clubs around the country and eventually around the world. Many still operate in much the same way as her original clubs. They are members-only and very exclusive."

"That sounds like something Gavin would admire."

"I haven't met her, but Ben and I have visited many of her clubs around the world. Like Gavin's, they are strictly neutral ground. And yes, very entertaining."

"Sounds like someone I'd really love to meet."

"She will adore you and probably try to get you to work for her." Tenzin stared at Chloe. "If she does, tell her that you are blood bound to Gavin. It's the only thing that might make her back off."

Well, that got intense quickly. "Okay." Chloe cleared her throat. "I'm sure we'll get along just fine, Tenzin. I wouldn't worry about..." She felt her phone buzzing in her pocket. "Oh look, my phone."

She pulled out her mobile and stared at the screen, surprised by the name that popped up.

Mother.

Chloe debated not answering the phone, but it must have been urgent in some way. She usually only spoke to her parents on major holidays and their birthdays.

She pressed the button to answer. "Hello, Mom. How are you?"

"Chloe?" Her mother cleared her throat. "I... I'm glad you answered. I didn't want to email, and sometimes you don't respond to my calls."

She frowned. Her mother sounded as if she'd been crying. "What's wrong?"

"I'm afraid it's your father. He's had a heart attack."

"What?" Chloe's knees gave out. Her bottom hit the chair. "Is he—?"

"I'm sorry, Chloe. He didn't survive."

Chloe's head began to swim, and she felt light-headed. "No."

"He went quickly. I wasn't able to..." Her mother cleared her throat again. "He's gone, Chloe. Your father is dead."

3

Gavin woke to the dark confines of his day chamber in his Garden District home. He'd bought it around the time he'd started his club in Houston, and he hadn't been disappointed with the purchase. It was a grand old manor that had been built by a wealthy shipping magnate in the nineteenth century.

He'd modified it for his own use, hired a trusted housekeeper, and used it every few years. When he wasn't in residence, he rented the space to Marie-Hélène for a reasonable price for guests she couldn't accommodate in her own compound.

Gavin glanced at his phone and saw a missed call from Chloe and two from Audra. "Cara, call Audra."

"Calling Audra, mobile."

The call went straight to her voice mail.

Gavin frowned. "Cara, call Dove."

"Calling Dove, mobile."

It was his nickname for his lover, and it was still jarring when he heard Cara, the polite AI helper in the Nocht system, call Chloe "Dove."

That call also went to voice mail.

Gavin stood. "Cara, do I have any voice mail messages?"

"You have... thirteen voice mail messages. Three from Veronica, three from Ben Vecchio, three from Audra, one from Chloe, one from Oleg, one from P-I-T-A, and one from Tenzin."

"Play voice mail from Chloe." His heart would be racing if he were human. As it was, his mind and body had settled into a cold, focused state that only happened when he was in danger.

Something was very wrong.

His lover's voice came through the speakers. "Hey, handsome. Uh... I'm *fine*. Okay? *I'm fine.* Something happened and I need to fly to LA. It's" —she cleared her throat— "stuff to do with my family, and just ignore all the other calls you're probably going to get, okay? Do your meeting, there's no rush, and I promise I am *fine*. I am not in any physical or mental danger. So do your thing, and just instead of flying back home, if you could meet me in LA, that would be better." She took a deep breath. "Love you, Gavin. Miss you. I'll see you tomorrow night."

Gavin was pacing when he spoke again. "Cara, play Audra's messages."

Audra's voice came on the line. "Hey, boss. Chloe is safe and not in any danger. She is telling me that she does not want me to tell you what is going on because I am in charge of her security, not her life." Audra huffed out a breath. "I think you should fly home."

There was a click, then Audra's voice returned. "Okay, don't fly home, fly to LA."

Another click. "We couldn't find a commercial flight until tomorrow, so Vecchio is sending his plane from LA along with an extra crew so they can land, pick us up and turn around."

"Are Ben and Tenzin going with you?" Gavin shouted at the speakers. "Fuck!"

"Ben and the crazy one are coming with us," Audra continued. "Tenzin was bitching about it for about half an hour, but Ben put his foot down, so she's on the plane with us."

"We own a fucking transport company," he yelled at the walls. "How could she not have found an available flight?"

Because Chloe would think nothing of flying commercial if he wasn't with her, and she probably wouldn't even put herself in first class. Ridiculous. And Veronica was with him, which meant that Chloe would take care of her own logistics.

Which she was perfectly capable of doing, but Gavin had security to think about, and commercial flights were anything but secure.

"Cara, play voice mail from Ben Vecchio." If someone didn't tell him what was going on, he was going to stab something.

"Hey, Gav, it's me. Chloe doesn't want me to call you but— Ow, fuck! Chloe, don't throw that." There was a scuffling sound, and the voice mail ended.

Ben's voice came back in the second message. "She's stronger than she looks. We're taking her to LA. I called Gio and he worked it all out."

Gavin didn't try to stop his snarl. It was his job to take care of Chloe, not Giovanni Fucking Vecchio's. He didn't care if the vampire had known his lover since she was young and treated her as family. Chloe was his.

Chloe's voice came through the line even though it

was Ben's number. "Gavin, like I said, ignore these people and just meet me in LA." She sounded annoyed. "Seriously, you guys. Just pack your shit and stop trying to interfere in my life. Gavin, I love you. See you in LA."

The annoyance in her voice actually comforted him.

"Cara, which voice mails are unplayed?"

"You have three voice mails from Veronica, one from Oleg, one from P-I-T-A, and one from Tenzin."

Gavin let out a slow breath. Veronica was staying in a room two floors above his, so he could check with her in person, he didn't need to talk to Oleg or his sister, so that just left...

"Cara, play voice mail from Tenzin."

The voice that came through the phone was halting. "It's me. Hmm. I think—I don't know if you want to know what I think, and I'm not going to tell you what's wrong because it is not my news to share."

Gavin closed his eyes and muttered, "Then why are you calling me, Tenzin?"

"You should fly to Los Angeles, but maybe not before your meetings, which I assume you are considering canceling at this point. We will land in that infernal machine just before dawn, so there is likely no way you will see Chloe before nightfall anyway."

Fuck. He hadn't considered that.

"So finish your meetings so you don't irritate Marie-Hélène, then have your humans fly you to Los Angeles during the day, and then you'll see her at nightfall."

Was he really taking scheduling advice from Tenzin? If he left New Orleans in an hour, he could be in Los Angeles when Chloe landed. Or could he?

Fuck, he was so turned around he couldn't think. Traveling across the Atlantic always disrupted his internal clock. Gavin threw on a pair of pants and a T-shirt, ignoring the pressed suit that was hanging right outside his day chamber. He stormed up the stairs and nearly ran into Veronica in the process.

She lifted both her hands. "I don't know what's going on either, but I am telling you right now that if we cancel this meeting with MHC, you might not get another chance to talk about the telecom project until next year because she will be very, very angry."

Gavin took a slow breath. "Explain."

Veronica slowly turned him around and pointed him back downstairs. "Stop. Think. Chloe and I spoke this afternoon—"

"What the fuck is going on?"

"I will only say that there has been a death in her family. She is upset, but she is in absolutely no danger. She's just very sad." Veronica continued nudging Gavin downstairs. "Trust me, Gavin. She knows how hard these things can be to coordinate, and she does not want you to cancel a meeting."

Gavin's heart sank when he heard that Chloe had lost someone in her family, but Veronica's practical advice was getting through. "This would be the third time we've canceled on Marie-Hélène."

"And she has rearranged her schedule multiple times to make the meeting tonight work," Veronica said. "So yes, if we cancel it at the last minute, she will border on livid. You know how mercurial she can be."

Gavin admired and respected the woman, but she could be highly volatile. He turned and faced Veronica. "She's fine?"

Veronica's eyes softened. "She's not fine; she's sad. But she is not in any *danger*, and canceling this meeting will not get you to her any faster." She tucked a strand of silver hair behind her ear and patted his shoulder. "Focus on your business. Semis will get you to Los Angeles by nightfall tomorrow, and she'll be there. I will fly commercial back to New York to take care of the house and Pete while both of you are gone."

He turned and walked back to his dressing room, growling under his breath. There were many advantages to being a vampire. He didn't age, his strength was enormous, and his elemental abilities had matured to the point where he could fly great distances swifter than the fastest bird.

But this was the literal dark side.

He couldn't meet his lover in Los Angeles to hold her in her grief because it would be daylight. He would be sleeping, and even if he wasn't, he couldn't expose himself to any kind of sunlight unless he had a death wish. Others would have to care for her in his absence, and it grated on him.

"I'll take the meeting tonight, but let MHC's people know we have one night to come to an understanding. They've seen the preliminary proposal—a night to hammer out details should be enough time."

Veronica nodded and shuffled some files in her arms. "Agreed, but I'll drop that in George's ear. The preliminaries have all been sent, and this isn't the first joint venture you and MHC have had. I don't think you're going to need more than a night."

MARIE-HÉLÈNE CLINKED her glass with Gavin's. "I like everything I am seeing and I believe this partnership could make us very rich. But, my love, like all new ventures, I need to know *why*."

Gavin's eyebrows went up. "Why?"

"Why is this necessary?" Marie-Hélène shrugged. "Nocht is efficient, widely adopted, and from all accounts, secure."

They were lounging in one of Marie-Hélène's salons. The velvet-covered walls were hung with impressionist nudes, the lamps were attuned to vampire eyes, and Gavin had taken off his jacket and draped it over the back of his chair when all their assistants and security finally left them alone.

They were waiting on signatures, and as expected, Marie-Hélène wanted a drink and a chat before she put a final pen to the contract. His hostess was sitting sideways on a chaise, her feet up, draped in a brilliant green silk caftan that brought out the gold flecks in her brown eyes.

"Think about what you just said. '*From all accounts*, secure.'" Gavin raised an eyebrow. "So it comes down to a question: How much do you trust Patrick Murphy?"

Her ruby lips turned up at the corners. "Hmmm. An excellent question."

The lamplight glowed off Marie-Hélène's brown skin and glistened on her hair, which was piled on her head in a mass of intricate braids. She made no attempt to hide the silver threads running through her braids. She looked like a vampire queen because she was. It was an unusual arrangement to have a neutral arbiter like Marie-Hélène Charmont as the vampire in charge, but in a city like New Orleans, which attracted a huge number of powerful vampire clans and rivals, it worked. She'd kept the peace for more than two hundred years.

"How much do I trust Patrick Murphy?" She tapped a finger to her plush lower lip.

In Gavin's opinion, Marie-Hélène had been turned when she was at her most stunning. Her face had aged to reflect her character—regal, confident, and playful.

Gavin leaned forward. "In order to access the voice software that Murphy developed, you have to give it access to your systems. To your messages, your files, your internet history. To everything. And while there hasn't been a security breach that I know of, there is no one but Patrick Murphy himself who can guarantee that his software isn't spying on outside systems." Gavin shrugged. "How much do we trust him? How much does anyone in our world trust him?"

Marie-Hélène sipped her blood-wine. "And you think we're more trustworthy?"

"We don't take sides, cher. We're not going to pull access to a software update because we're in a trade dispute like Murphy might. We're not going to spy on a rival company because we have no rivals."

"You make an excellent point."

"People already trust us to host meetings, negotiate disputes, and provide safe haven and safe drinking. And while I don't believe there will ever be a vampire who trusts electronic communication completely, it has improved business and our ability to assimilate into the human world. For the two of us to create a system like Nocht—"

"Both devices and hardware?"

"It *has* to be both. Right now Nocht is running vampire-friendly software on mostly human devices. They're cumbersome. Unattractive. We can do better."

He'd taken the idea to another ally in Brussels, but

while they were interested in developing the software, the hardware didn't excite them. Gavin was insistent that the hardware and software had to be developed in tandem, so he backed out of the deal.

Marie-Hélène narrowed her eyes. "I do worry about the scale."

"We scale slowly." He reassured her. "Make these devices and this security a *premium* option in a Nocht-dominant world. We don't want to be a bargain, Marie-Hélène. We want to be the very secure *upgrade*." Gavin sat back. It was the last pitch he had, and he knew it would work. Marie-Hélène adored finding the exclusive, the unique, and the finest. Whether it was humans or art, she only wanted the best. "This will be luxury technology, and who knows luxury better than you and me?"

She offered him a slow smile. "You've convinced me. Should we put our names on it?"

"We don't have to put our names on the company, but we shouldn't make a secret of our ownership. Our reputations will be part of the selling point."

"Agreed." She leaned forward and clinked his glass with her own. "To another successful venture."

"To us and to the future."

"And to money."

Gavin smiled. "That part is always welcome." He and Marie-Hélène appreciated money the way that only those raised dirt-poor could. "You're going to be very happy with this, my friend. I know part of your conditions was basing the venture here in New Orleans, and I'm looking forward to spending time here."

Marie-Hélène laughed. "Does that mean I will finally meet your darling little human? I watched her performance the other night. Absolutely exquisite. To see that silhouette en pointe." She kissed her fingertips. "It thrills me."

"I didn't know they were broadcasting it." He'd caught the premiere just before he had to leave for Paris. "She's stunning, isn't she?"

"The theater does live broadcasts of events for certain patrons, and yes, she is exquisite. The *life* in her movement. The grace and the expression. I could not take my eyes off her. It's no wonder you've found yourself so enamored." She reached over and patted his hand. "It's good for you to have a partner. I still miss my Gerard. Every night, I wake and hope to see him, but he is not there." Her face held a soft sadness. "I am so happy for your joy."

"Thank you, Marie." Gavin finished his glass of wine and set it down. "Chloe has enjoyed this show immensely. Absolutely enamored with the choreographer, but I'm sure she'll be excited to visit your city as well. I don't know that she's ever been."

"I will make her my most personal friend." Marie-Hélène beamed. "She will be the toast of the city."

Gavin wasn't sure Chloe would be interested in Marie-Hélène's level of patronage, but that would be up to his lover to decide. He glanced at the crystal-trimmed clock on the wall. "I need to let you know I cannot stay longer than three this morning. I need to fly to Los Angeles as soon as we're finished."

Her eyebrows went up. "Oh?"

"There has been a death in the family," Gavin said. "Chloe's family. It just happened, and I don't have all the details, but I'm needed there."

Marie-Hélène leaned forward and placed her hand

over Gavin's. "Of course you're needed! Why didn't you go immediately?"

"Her plane won't land until the morning, and I didn't want to delay our meeting any more than necessary since we've had to reschedule so many times."

"But Gavin, if you're needed..." Marie-Hélène was clearly flattered by Gavin's devotion. "I would never be angry with you."

Of course you would. He smiled. "You're too generous."

"But I am sad to see you leave my beautiful city so quickly!" Marie-Hélène's eyes were plaintive. "When she has recovered from her loss, you must bring her to me. After all, one day we will be family, *non*?"

Gavin held up a finger. "If she so chooses, Marie-Hélène. And only then."

Long ago, Marie-Hélène had been on the verge of losing a woman who was as dear to her as a daughter. It had been tuberculosis, and Marie-Hélène had been out of the country on business when Chantelle had taken a grave turn.

At Marie-Hélène's request, Gavin had been the one to turn her. He'd then relinquished all rights to the new vampire as a sire and turned her over to Marie-Hélène's aegis with the understanding that if he were ever in the same position, she would do the same for him.

Chantelle might technically be his daughter, but in Gavin's mind, she had only ever been Marie-Hélène's.

"How is Chance?" He tried to distract his old friend from Chloe. "I haven't heard from her in some time. I know she's busy."

"She's wonderful. Did she write to you when she moved?"

"She did. Is she still enjoying the horse farm?"

"We both are," Marie-Hélène said. "When I want quiet, all I need is to visit my darling girl and I am refreshed. It's so beautiful there."

"I'm glad she's happy." Gavin didn't consider Chantelle his in any way, but there was a blood tie that neither of them could deny, though it was completely hidden from the immortal world. "And I promise, when and if Chloe—"

"But she must." Marie-Hélène leaned forward. "Why would she not, Gavin?"

He was silent because he had no answer. It was the one thing about his life that haunted him. Gavin had found real love and belonging with a partner. He'd found a woman he actually wanted to spend eternity with.

And she was still undecided about immortality.

"It's not about me," he said. "It's about this life."

Was it though?

"Of course," Marie-Hélène said. "I would never try to pressure her. It's just..." Her eyes showed her age. "It is a dangerous world, is it not?"

"So we try to make it a little less." Gavin leaned down to kiss her cheek. "Bid me farewell, my friend. I need to leave."

4

Chloe slept on the plane even though she was sure she wouldn't. She wanted to dissolve into thin air and disappear. She hated when people fussed over her, and now she had two overprotective humans and two overprotective vampires.

But all she wanted was Gavin.

It had taken everything in her not to beg him to come home. She knew how complicated it had been to find a time to meet with Marie-Hélène, and Chloe didn't want Gavin to resent taking time from his business so she could cry on his shoulder.

Not that he would blame her. He wouldn't. But she would know that she'd interfered with an important meeting, and there was no need for it.

She blinked awake, the events of the night before clear as daylight in her mind. By the time dusk had fallen and Ben had roused from his day rest, Tenzin had already spoken to Beatrice, who'd immediately sent a plane to New York to pick Chloe up even though she insisted she could fly commercial.

Audra was no help with that one; Audra hated to fly commercial.

They boarded an hour after nightfall and were in the air by the time Gavin woke in another time zone. They would fly for over five hours to get to Los Angeles, leaving plenty of time for them to get to Ben's family home before dawn.

Chloe couldn't bear the thought of knocking on her mother's door at three in the morning. She didn't even know if she would stay at her parents' house when they arrived. If she did, Gavin would have to stay somewhere else. Her mother and father knew nothing about the vampire world.

Her mother. Her mother was the only one now. Her father had died never really knowing who Gavin was.

"Chloe, can I get you anything?" Audra gently touched her shoulder. "Steve just lay down to sleep. We've got about two more hours before we land."

"I'm fine."

"You can't be fine."

But she was. Or rather, she felt frozen. Nothing seemed real, and she didn't know how to make sense of the emotions ricocheting around her head. It wasn't as if she and her father were close. She had never been a daddy's girl. Her father was a clinical, precise man who was—

Had been. He *had been* one of the best oncologists in Southern California after seeing his mother waste away from bone cancer when he was only sixteen.

Chloe often wondered if her father's empathy and softness had died when he lost his mother. His relationship with Chloe's mother had felt more like a partnership to produce superior offspring than any kind of relationship. They were both physicians with stellar reputations and phenomenal professional success, her mother in cardiology and her father in oncology.

John Washington Reardon and Clara Brown-Reardon had one child, and to them she was an utter disappointment.

Chloe.

She turned to Audra. "I'm fine. I promise. I ate something when we boarded."

"Are you drinking enough? After my mom passed, I had headaches for days and I thought they were related just to the grief, but I hadn't been drinking anything."

Chloe raised a bottle of water. "I'm good. Promise."

And she wasn't grieving. Chloe didn't know what that meant or what grief should look like when the parent who died had treated her as if she was an embarrassment for over ten years.

The Doctors Reardon had never seen Chloe's career as a dancer with anything but disdain. Dancing wasn't a profession—it was a hobby.

Her practice meant nothing. Her discipline meant nothing. Dancing in off-Broadway shows wasn't a serious job that would impress their intellectual friends or contribute to the betterment of the world, and that was all that mattered to them.

While their friends' children were following their parents into medical school, or at the very least law school, Chloe had packed up her stuff and moved to New York to live in a shitty third-floor walk-up apartment with three other girls, usher at theaters that wouldn't hire her, and fall into an abusive relationship with a finance bro.

She closed her eyes. Fuck. No wonder her parents never took her seriously.

The abusive relationship might have been in the past, but from her parents' perspective, Chloe had just traded one rich boyfriend for another. They'd met Gavin, but they were unimpressed to hear that he owned an entertainment group that included clubs, theaters, and bars around the world.

Had he gone to college?

Did he have a degree?

What did his parents do?

All those questions Gavin had fielded with as much grace as possible, but Chloe couldn't bring herself to subject him to their interrogations more than a few times over the five years they'd been together.

Audra settled next to her. "We'll land in Burbank; that's the fastest airport to get you home."

"Yep. Ben told you I'm staying at his place, right? His uncle's place? At least when we first get there."

"Yes."

Of course, her parents only lived about a mile from Ben's aunt and uncle.

Her mother lived there. Not her father. Not anymore.

She closed her eyes and took a deep breath. "Has anyone heard from Gavin?"

"We can't get any signal in here," Audra said. "With the insulation they use to customize these for vampires—"

"Right." Chloe nodded. "I knew that."

She did know that; her brain was just mush.

Your father is dead.

When was the last time she'd talked to him? His birthday? Probably. What had they talked about? Chloe couldn't even remember it that clearly. He'd mentioned a sport-fishing trip with friends. Said something about his

34

partner's son graduating from Johns Hopkins. Or was it a residency? It had been months.

Chloe tried to think of her most positive memories of her father, but her mind was coming up blank. Dance recitals? When she was little, he'd sometimes been at her dance recitals if he wasn't working. When she was *very* little, he'd greeted her at the end of a recital with flowers.

Little girls in tutus were adorable. Teenage daughters pursuing "foolish dreams" weren't so charming. Her father had been the one to make it clear: she went to college for a respectable field of study that contributed to the greater good, or she got nothing when she left their home.

Nothing.

Not an allowance. Not health insurance. Not even the cell phone that she'd paid for on their plan.

Chloe left anyway, and despite their lack of support, she managed. Sure, she had to rely on her friends for a lot, but she wasn't too proud for that. What she *was* too proud for was asking her parents for a damn thing.

I'm sorry, Chloe. He didn't survive.

She should mourn. She should cry. There should be grief.

But how did you mourn a relationship that already felt dead?

THEY'D RENOVATED the kitchen even though neither of them cooked.

"It looks good," Chloe said. "That refrigerator is huge."

"The real estate agent recommended it."

Chloe turned to her mother. "Are you moving?"

"We were. We were going to downsize. Now?" Her mother shook her head slightly. "I don't know."

Clara Brown-Reardon was wearing a neat grey suit and going through the cards attached to the flowers and ferns that were starting to deluge the house. She wouldn't wear black until her husband's service, but then she'd wear grey, navy, and other muted colors for around a year after. That's what she'd done when her own mother died at age sixty-five from a massive and very unexpected stroke.

And now she'd lost her husband to a heart attack.

"Did Dad know—?"

"No. He had a stress test three months ago with no signs of disease. There was no reason to do an angiogram." She blinked. "There was no *apparent* reason to do an angiogram."

Because there had been a reason; her mother just hadn't known it.

"Mom, if he wasn't showing symptoms—"

"I'm very aware that this isn't my fault."

Are you? Chloe would never say it out loud.

Clara set down the stack of envelopes. "I'm surprised your boyfriend isn't with you. He seemed very... attentive."

Attentive was her mother's way of saying possessive.

"He's coming tonight. I told him to finish his business in New Orleans before he came out. He was in Paris a couple of nights ago, then he had a meeting in New Orleans, then he was heading home. I didn't think there was any reason for him to cancel the meeting since it was complicated to set up."

36

"Very practical." Clara nodded, seeming to approve. "I'm surprised the Vecchio boy didn't come with you."

"He'll be here with Gavin." *Because the sun would burn him up. Oh, by the way, did I mention my first boyfriend is a vampire now? No? And my current one is too.* "My friends Zain and Audra were fine driving me over here."

Chloe had forgotten what it felt like to hide so many things from regular people. Most of her friends in New York were either vampires, vampire adjacent, or theater people who never questioned anyone who only came outside at night.

"Do you want me to call anyone?" Chloe looked around at the perfect palace where she'd grown up. Other than the kitchen remodel, not much had changed. "Did you call everyone back East?"

"I called your aunt Sunny, so your father's entire family knows. God knows that woman loves to share dramatic news." Clara pursed her lips. "I shouldn't be ungracious. Auntie Sheila is already making arrangements to fly out. She'll get in touch with everyone on my side."

Her mother had been born in Nashville, the daughter of a math professor at Fisk University and a schoolteacher. Her father was from Georgia, the first in his family to go to college, though Chloe's grandfather had been a well-known pastor in the African Methodist Episcopal Church. Her parents had met at UCLA medical school and made their home in California ever since; all of Chloe's cousins were from back East, and she barely knew them.

Clara looked up and crossed her arms over her chest. "There's not much to do right now."

That was her mother's worst nightmare. Dr. Clara Brown-Reardon was a singularly busy person. Work, school committees, alumni associations, professional women's associations. Chloe couldn't remember her mother ever being idle.

"Are there any pictures you want to look through?" Chloe tried to remember the last funeral she'd attended in her family. It had been for her father's oldest brother, who'd died in a car accident a few years before. She'd barely known him, but her parents had requested she attend. "When Uncle James passed, his kids put together that beautiful slideshow with all their—"

"Your father hated that maudlin presentation." Clara's mouth twisted. "He forbade me from doing anything like that. We talked about it on the flight home after the service."

No doubt her father would have thought a slideshow of family pictures was too sentimental. Too common.

Besides, what kind of family pictures did they have? Nothing but the formal portrait they'd taken for Christmas every year until Chloe was eighteen and left home. They didn't do road trips or family vacations. Her parents had vacationed separately for years on account of their busy schedules.

Chloe sighed. "Okay, so no slideshow."

Her mother was staring out the window. "There will be songs, and I'm sure a few people will want to speak. Many of his patients kept in touch, and I've no doubt Scott will be contacting them."

"Have June and Scott come by?" Scott Bogosian was her father's partner. "What about Dad's friends from the club?" She remembered her mother's partner. She'd always assumed the two women were friends. "Where's Ronnie?"

"I'm sure once she's finished covering my patients, she'll go home, Chloe." Clara sounded irritated. "Everyone knows." Clara walked to a drawer near the back door and opened it. "What should we order for lunch? I don't feel like cooking."

Because your husband just died.

Chloe couldn't help but be irritated. If all her parents' friends knew her father had died, where were they? She'd been surrounded by friends from the moment she'd gotten the call from her mother until Zain and Audra had dropped her off by the front door.

They were still outside, Audra keeping an eye on the back of the house while Zain watched the front.

Chloe had walked into an empty mansion while her mother had been writing thank-you notes for the flowers that had shown up. Not even the housekeeper was here.

"The service will be at First AME, probably the middle of next week. I'm thinking Wednesday should be a respectable amount of time. His family from Georgia will want to come out."

"What about yours?"

"I already told you Sheila is coming. I'm sure whoever is able will fly out as their schedules allow." Clara stared at a stack of menus. "Anyway, what do you want to eat?" For the first time in Chloe's memory, her mother seemed listless. It wasn't like her to simply ask—usually she'd have her top three selections already chosen and ask Chloe to pick from those.

"What do you want?"

Clara paged through the stack of menus. "Honestly, I don't care. I'm not hungry, but I know I need to eat."

ELIZABETH HUNTER

"Do you and Dad—?" Chloe stopped herself. "I mean, do you still like Celestino? We could order something. I'm sure Zain would be happy to go pick it up."

"Who is he?" Clara frowned. "Never mind, it's fine. Just order some things. I'll eat later. I think I want to take a nap." She set the menus in front of Chloe and walked toward the hallway. "Are you going to stay here or at the Vecchios' while you're in town?"

Chloe didn't know what to say. "Why don't Gavin and I stay at the Vecchios'? That way when Auntie Sheila comes, she can stay with you."

Clara nodded. "She may bring her girls with her, and one of them just had a baby, so that'll be fine."

"Okay." Chloe felt vestigial, like an extra finger or an appendix. She was there, but no one seemed to know why. "I'll stay here while you're sleeping in case there are any more deliveries."

"Thank you, Chloe." Her mother touched her shoulder as she passed her on the way to the stairs. "Your father was talking about flying to New York for your most recent show. I'm sorry we didn't do that. He said it was at Lincoln Center?"

"Yeah." Chloe felt like her mother had slapped her. "Our company was part of the spring dance series."

And they were thinking about attending? Nothing in the previous ten years had prepared Chloe to hear that, but her mother had dropped that information like it was an interesting bit of trivia at a cocktail party.

"Lincoln Center is quite impressive." Her mother walked past her, then turned at the foot of the stairs. "Were you a principal?"

She blinked and returned to reality. "No, Mom. I was just in the company."

40

"Still... that's something."

"Yeah." She looked down at the stack of menus and tried to muster up an appetite.

This was going to be a very long week.

~

SHE WAS SLEEPING upright in her mother's front room when someone touched her shoulder. Chloe opened her eyes and saw the only face in the world she wanted.

"Gavin." Immediately her eyes began to water, and her throat grew tight. It was as if a dam had broken in her chest. She heaved a cry out, grabbed him around the neck, and clung.

"There, dove." He wrapped her tightly and rocked back and forth. "Tell me, Chloe. I'm here."

The words erupted from her throat, and her eyes burned with all the tears she'd been holding back. "My dad is dead, Gavin."

"Och, love." He held her tighter. "I'm sorry, Chloe. I'm so very sorry."

"He died and he was going to fly out to see me dance at Lincoln Center but he didn't and now he died." She knew she wasn't making much sense, but she also knew he'd figure it out.

"I'm sorry, dove." He kept rocking her back and forth. "I'm so sorry he's gone."

It was shit. Her dad was dead, and everything was awful.

But Gavin was back.

5
———————

Gavin watched her from the doorway and spoke into the phone. "Aye, she's sleeping now. So is her mother. I don't think she was planning to stay here tonight, but part of me doesn't want to wake her and move her."

Ben was on the other end of the call. "Zain can stay there if you need him with Audra."

"I'll send one of my people to relieve Zain; I've already talked to Audra." But Gavin would need to leave before sunrise, which irritated him.

He owned two clubs in Los Angeles and had numerous safe places he could stay, but it wasn't one of his usual territories, which meant he felt exposed.

And Chloe was doubly exposed.

She was grieving her father—not that the man deserved her tears—and was distracted by her mother. She was out of her element and vulnerable as hell. Gavin wanted to lock her away, but that wasn't possible.

He heard a door open and turned to see Clara watching him from the other side of the upstairs landing.

"Ben," Gavin said quietly. "I'll call you back."

"Take care of her."

"I will." He slid his bulky phone into his pocket and turned to Chloe's mother. "Dr. Brown-Reardon. It's good to see you, but I'm very sorry for the circumstances."

"Gavin." Clara had been sleeping when he arrived at dusk. "Chloe said you had business in New Orleans to take care of. I hope that went well."

"I signed papers late last night, traveled here during the day. I'm sorry I wasn't able to come with Chloe."

"It's fine." She turned toward the stairs and started toward the first floor. "Leave her to sleep. I could tell she was tired earlier, and I'm sure she has jet lag."

He glanced over his shoulder, but he suspected Clara was correct. Chloe was dead to the world. "Can I make you a cup of tea?"

She smirked a little. "Sure. Tea. That's the British answer to everything, right?"

"It's the Scottish one anyway." He followed Clara down the stairs and into the kitchen. "And if tea doesn't work, we'll get the whisky out."

"I'm not much of a whisky drinker, so hopefully the tea will cure this headache." She pressed her fingers to her temple. "I'm probably dehydrated."

"Tea is definitely the remedy then." Gavin walked past her and saw an electric kettle on the counter.

Bollocks.

If he was very careful, he might not short it out.

The Reardons' new kitchen was a veritable minefield of electronic hazards. It would likely be impossible for him to spend much time in the room and not start a small electrical fire with his amnis, so he'd have to be cautious.

He filled the kettle at the sink, then keeping his back

to Clara, used a wooden spoon to press the power button, letting out a small sigh of relief when there was no accompanying spark.

"Where do you keep your tea?"

"We don't have much, but there are some bags to the left of the sink in that top cupboard."

Gavin searched and found a pathetic selection of small paper bags on a shelf above carefully-lined-up coffee mugs. "Will your family be coming soon?"

"My sister will." Clara crossed her arms and leaned on the counter. "I'm sure John's sister will too. His older brother passed a few years ago."

"I remember."

Clara nodded. "So there's not as much family on that side. But my sister will come."

"I'm glad. It's not good to be alone during these times."

Clara examined him. "Do you come from a big family?"

Mortal or immortal?

"About average size for the area where I grew up." *A mad, batty vampire with self-image issues.* "I've a sister who lives in France with her children. Works in winemaking."

There. That was enough information to seem normal, wasn't it?

"And your parents?"

"Oh, they passed long ago," Gavin said.

But wait, he looked like he was barely older than Chloe.

"There was an auto accident," he added quickly. "Very sudden... Uh, very sad." He was going to have to remember to tell Chloe this entire backstory because her mother didn't trust him, and he was sure she'd cross-check everything with her daughter. "So it's just my sister and me these days."

"And she works in wine production and you have bars?"

He sighed. "I have a number of bars around the world, but I have more clubs. Entertainment clubs, night-clubs, social clubs. That sort of thing."

"Chloe doesn't talk much about your business, but I know you travel a lot."

So does your daughter, which you'd know if you called her more than two times a year. "Chloe is a wonderful partner for countless reasons, but one of the benefits of her job is that when she doesn't have a show in production, her work usually allows her to travel with me. It's been quite wonderful."

"Huh." Clara watched him as he removed the tea bags and doctored the Earl Grey.

"How do you take your tea?" Gavin asked.

"However you make it is fine."

"Very well." He added two spoons of sugar and a hefty dollop of milk. "There you are."

"Thank you." Clara sipped from her mug. "My daughter seems to have all sorts of people watching her these days. I know she said the young man who dropped her off and the older woman are friends, but I can spot private security."

Gavin said nothing.

Clara looked him dead in the eye. "Are you a criminal, Mr. Wallace?"

How could he possibly answer that honestly? There were countless actions he'd taken in the previous 160-odd years that would probably classify him as a criminal in her eyes, but none of them were the reason that Chloe had to be guarded so carefully.

"What I am," he said carefully, "is very rich. And very influential in certain circles."

It was Clara's turn to be quiet.

"None of my business involves anything as tawdry or dangerous as drugs or weapons or smuggling. Nothing of the sort. Most of it is quite boring. But because of my properties, I could be a target for any number of dangerous people who would love to have leverage over me." He nodded toward the stairs. "There is no human being in the world I care more about than your daughter, Dr. Brown-Reardon. It's not very likely someone would target her, but it's possible."

"That's why you have guards on her?"

"Yes, and it's very likely that I will put even more guards on her while she's in Los Angeles. This isn't her home anymore, and there are subtle ways she will be at a disadvantage that would not be an issue if she were in New York."

Clara sniffed. "Well, I suppose if she's going to be with a bar owner, it's good that he's a rich one."

Gavin bit his tongue for the hundredth time. In their limited interactions, Chloe's mother always managed to passive-aggressively insinuate that he wasn't good enough for her daughter, that her daughter was wasting her life in New York, and that her daughter had squandered her intellect.

The one time he'd tried to push back, Chloe hadn't liked it, so he stopped. Now he tried to ignore the digs and focus on what mattered—Chloe.

"I'll talk to her about it so she knows, but if you see increased security around the house while she's here, that is why." Gavin shrugged. "They won't likely need to come inside unless there's an emergency."

"Lovely." Clara pursed her lips and slipped off the barstool. "I'm going upstairs. Are you staying with us while you're in town?"

Not unless you have vampire safe rooms I don't know about.

"I've committed to staying with some friends while I'm here. I'm not sure what Chloe's plans are, but I assume she'll need to stay close for family reasons."

"She'll probably stay with the Vecchios," Clara muttered. "Strange family, but she always liked them. You know she and Ben dated in high school?"

"I've heard. Did you know Ben's married now?"

Clara's eyebrows went up. "No."

This should be amusing. "I believe it was a traditional ceremony overseas. You should ask him about it. I hear the pictures are lovely."

~

Chloe was curled up against his chest, lying in her childhood bedroom. "You told her they were *married*?"

"Yes." Gavin smiled. "That should rankle Tenzin thoroughly."

"Do you purposefully try to make life harder for Ben?"

"Of course I do. I thought that was obvious."

Her shoulders shook slightly. "I think I'm jet-lagged."

"I think you are too." He twisted one of her curls around his finger. "I'm going to have to leave soon. Do you want to come with me or stay here?"

She sighed and hugged his arms around her more

47

tightly. "I should probably stay here. As soon as you're out for the day, I'm just going to have to come back here and be with her."

"You don't, actually. If she makes you feel worse about your father passing, you don't have to spend time with her."

"She's my mom, Gavin."

She's the woman who gave birth to you, who has subsequently discouraged every action you've taken in your life to make yourself happy and pursue success on your own terms.

He kissed her shoulder. "I know, dove."

"We don't have the greatest relationship, but I don't want her to be alone."

"When is her sister coming?"

"Today."

"Good." He nodded. "So you stay here today and then tonight you can spend the night with me, Ben, and Tenzin at the Vecchios'. Be around people who love you." *Unlike the unsupportive wench in the other wing of this castle.* "How does that sound?"

"Let me see how things are when my auntie Sheila comes."

"Is this the Sheila who came to see your performance last summer?"

"Yes."

"I like her." Gavin frowned. "She's your mother's sister?"

"Don't act so shocked."

"She has an excellent sense of humor. What happened to your mother?"

Chloe huffed out a laugh. "You've got me. Sheila studied psychiatry and Clara studied biology? I have no idea. I think my mom just takes after her father, and from what I can tell, he wasn't the warmest person."

Gavin tried to remember his parents, but the memories were so fuzzy as to be nearly gone. "I think I took after my mother. I remember my father criticizing me about that."

"Why would he criticize that?"

"I don't think it was considered very admirable for a young man to take after his mother in my community. I left home quite early. Probably because of that."

"You don't remember?"

He leaned over and nibbled behind her ear. "I am a very old man, dove." His hand slid around her waist and pulled her back against the length of his body so her beautifully round ass was nestled right where he liked it.

"You don't seem that old to me." She wiggled her bottom into him, and Gavin let out a groan.

He growled. "You know what I've been missing, don't you?"

"It's been a week and a half since I've seen you," Chloe said. "Which seems like forever right now." She reached around and grabbed his wrist, placing his hand directly on her left breast. "And I'm fine, so—"

"No." He scooted down and began to pepper kisses along her neck. "I know you're not fine, so I want you to stop saying it."

She turned and captured his mouth with her lips. "I'll be more fine if you make love to me." She shifted in bed, turning to face him, and stretched one leg over his. "And please do not hold back because you think I'm fragile."

Gavin looked in her eyes and knew she was hurting, but he also knew he could make her feel better even if it was just for a few moments.

He brushed back a curl that had escaped from her high ponytail. "I'd take this sadness from you if I could."

She blinked. "Would amnis take it away?"

"It could make you forget for a while," he said quietly. "But then someone would tell you and it would hurt all over again. There is no antidote for grief but living or dying, and you're not allowed to do the latter." He took her mouth in a long kiss.

No dying. Not ever. Stay with me, Chloe.

Gavin slipped his hand under her shirt and slowly drew it up and over her body. It was spring in Southern California, and the days were warmer than New York. The light cotton T-shirt fell to the ground, followed by Chloe's joggers and the delicate lace panties he'd bought her for Christmas.

Most of her lingerie was his own purchases now. He delighted in covering her delicious curves in bright colors, lace, and silk. He ran his fingertips over the rise of her bottom and felt the shiver travel up her spine. Her nipples perked against his chest.

"You still have a suit on," she said against his lips. "Not fair."

"What do you mean?" He sat up against her headboard, lifting her onto his lap. "I took my jacket off."

She smiled and spread her hands across his chest, teasing the buttons that tracked down his chest. "How proper of you, Mr. Wallace."

"Och, nae me, lass. Nowt but a simple barman here."

Chloe's face lit up when she laughed, and Gavin knew he'd do anything, spare nothing, and break every rule to keep her with him for eternity.

He trailed a single finger from her lips, down her

neck, between her breasts, and over her belly. "Unbutton my pants for me, will you, dove?"

"Yes." Deft fingers loosened his pants, spread them, and withdrew his hardened cock, which was begging for attention. She gripped his erection in one small hand.

Fuck, he was her servant. She could ask him to do anything and he'd beg to say yes.

"Up now." He lifted her bottom with both hands, nudging her up and onto his cock.

She sank down slowly, her strong legs giving her exquisite control.

"God above." He let his head fall back, knocking it against the headboard. "Fuck."

She leaned forward and put her arms around his neck. "That sounds like an excellent idea."

"Fuck?"

"Yes please."

He thrust up as she lowered herself, and her breath caught in her throat. "Say please again."

She arched her back and drew his head down to taste her breasts. "Please, Mr. Wallace."

His mouth closed over one nipple and sucked hard. He'd left bruises, but she never complained. Chloe knew how tightly Gavin had to control his strength when he made love to her. Every now and then, he loosened the leash a little and she loved it.

His fangs grew long as his cock grew harder. He scraped his teeth over the delicate skin of her neck and breasts.

"Please what, dove?" Gavin moved his mouth to the other nipple and teased his tongue over the tip.

Her breath was coming faster and harder. His fingers found the top of her sex and teased the heated flesh that begged for attention. Torturously slow circles always made her come, so he moved his thumb as gently as possible.

"Please." She was nearly crying. "Fuck me."

His mouth released her breast. "And?"

She pressed his mouth to her neck. "Bite me."

He nearly came just hearing it. He thrust up again, her hips and her breasts bouncing as she rode his cock. "And?" His fangs scraped along her collarbone.

"Make me come."

Done. He pressed in with his thumb and allowed his amnis to shiver across her skin, kissing it with a thousand tiny pricks of pleasure as he bent his knees up and thrust into her, driving his cock deeper into her body.

She rode him for mindless minutes, their bodies joined, and his soul settled.

Stay with me.

Stay forever.

Stay in the darkness and be my light.

Just as she reached the precipice of pleasure, he bit, clasping his hand over her mouth to muffle her cries of pleasure.

He pulled hard from her vein to increase the sensation as they both came. He closed his eyes and saw lightning for a few brief seconds before he forced himself to close the wounds so he didn't take too much.

He held her as she rode out her orgasm, her skin alive with sensation and her lips flushed and red from his kiss.

Queen.

Fuck him, she was glorious. He was glorious. They were glorious together. He wanted her to fly. He wanted to make love to her in the middle of a rainstorm with the air alive with electricity. He wanted to strip her naked and put her on a throne so he could kiss her knees, spread her legs, and devour her sex.

When it came to Chloe, Gavin was deranged.

His lover was naked and draped against his chest. "You hardly drank."

"I fed before I came." He ran his hands up and down her spine. "You don't need to be tired tomorrow."

"I don't mind. I like it."

He smiled. "I know, but if I don't take too much, I can bite you tomorrow night too."

She let out a contented sigh. "Good point."

"Do you think your mother heard us?"

"It's a massive house, so probably not. And I don't really care if she did." She laid her head on his shoulder. "We've been together over five years, Gavin. I'm pretty sure she knows we have sex."

"Fuck me, has it been five years?"

"Mm-hmm." She stretched like a lazy cat.

"Five years though?"

"Really and truly." She sat up. "I should go and clean up."

He clamped a hand on her backside, forcing her to stay. "We should get married."

She reared back, her eyes wide. "What did you just say?"

Oh fuck, that had just popped out.

From where, Gavin had no idea.

6

"*We should talk about it later.*"

Chloe kept going over and over it in her head.

Gavin had left her with those words and disappeared to whatever light-safe room he was using for the day, so they couldn't continue the conversation. Audra was Gavin's employee, so talking to her was out. Beatrice had always had issues with Gavin, and Tenzin was at the Vecchios' house.

Which left Zain.

The man scratched the dark brown beard that covered his face. "You sure you want to talk to me about this? You don't have any girls you can talk to about this shit?"

"Who am I going to get advice from, Zain? Tenzin?" She pointed to the house. "My mother? My aunt? People who have no idea vampires even exist?"

"I'm just saying..." He sighed. "Okay, talk."

She and Zain had become friends when they went to Ethiopia the year before as part of Tenzin and Ben's entourage—two Americans in Addis Ababa, scoping things out and filling their days when the vampires were sleeping.

Lots of people mistook them for a couple, but Zain had been dating a regular human for a little over a year. He felt a lot more like a big brother than anything else. Not that she had a big brother, but Zain was kind of what she imagined for a big brother. Big, strong, steady. He knew about fixing cars, and he gave good advice.

So she'd cornered him in the front yard after lunch.

"I'm probably not a good person to talk to about this," he started, "because I have made a point to never get involved with an immortal." He reached over his shoulders and tied his locs back with a black bandanna.

"Why not?"

He crossed his arms over his chest. "Just don't see a future in it. I want a family, kids, T-ball and peewee football. All that shit. Not in the cards with a vampire."

"Fair." She stared at his arms. His biceps looked like they'd expanded to the size of small soccer balls. "Have you been working out more?"

"It's a constant process, sis. I gotta keep up with immortal threats. Brute strength is about all I got with my build." He sighed again and leaned forward, bracing his elbows on his knees. "Okay, so the vampire you have been living with for five years now wants to get married. Do you have some philosophical objection to the institution?"

"He has literally never mentioned it before now. That's why I'm freaking out."

"And you're extra emotional because of your father."

"Yeah. So why did he bring it up now?"

"I don't know, Chloe." He huffed out a breath. "Thinking about life. Thinking about death. Thinking about the passage of time. Hell, half the shit men say—immortal or not—isn't thought out in advance. Unless you're a player like Giovanni Vecchio and you don't hardly say shit, some stuff is just gonna slip out. I can almost promise that idea just popped into his damn head."

"So you don't think he meant it?" Did that feel worse? Chloe couldn't decide if that felt worse.

"I didn't say that." Zain squinted. "I mean, if it hadn't been on his mind at all, he wouldn't have said it. So... the idea was floating around somewhere. What's the deal? You've been together a long time. You rethinking things?"

"No. Gavin and I are happy."

"So what's the issue?"

Chloe racked her brain. What *was* the issue? "I didn't think he wanted to get married. He's not religious."

"Well, I guess he's thinking about it. So you gotta decide what you think about it now."

She looked over her shoulder at the house that was slowly filling with more people by the hour. Chloe and Zain had picked Sheila and her two daughters up from the airport. Her aunt Sunny took a taxi from LAX. The house was occupied by more and more relatives as the extended family descended on Pasadena.

Chloe couldn't wait to leave. "I don't know any of these people."

He sat up straight. "You want to go?"

She looked at the house, at the rental cars parked in the driveway, at Audra's nondescript sedan. "Is Gavin at the Vecchios'?"

"You'd have to ask Audra. I am not on his staff. But you know you always got a place at Giovanni's. He and

Beatrice were nearly snarling last night when Ben didn't bring you back."

"Yeah, they know my parents." There was a hollow spot in her chest. "My father is dead."

Zain pressed his lips together. "I know it wasn't easy between the two of you. I'm sorry."

"I don't know how to feel. I'm sad. It..." She struggled to find the words. "It hurts, but I'm angry too. I was trying to call up nice memories we had together, and I can't think of anything, Zain. Maybe it's because I'm not thinking clearly right now."

"Maybe." He kept his voice soft. "But sometimes the family you're born to isn't the one that fits, and there's nothing wrong with that."

She nodded. "But that means the one you find..." She looked at him. "That makes it extra important, right? Because those are the people who chose you."

"That's one way of looking at it."

She looked over her shoulder at the house of people who didn't know her. "I didn't want my mom to be alone."

"I can respect that," he said. "But she's not alone now, and if there's ever a time when I think it's okay to be selfish, it's when you've lost someone important to you. And whether you liked him or not, your dad was important. He had a big place in your life, and you need to honor that."

She took a deep breath and let it out slowly. "I'm going to go get my bag packed; then I want to go to the Vecchios'."

"You got it. I'll let Audra know."

SHE COULDN'T SAY her mother had been pleased that she was leaving, but she definitely wasn't surprised. Her cousins all acted shocked, but most of them knew the score. She arrived at the Vecchios' in the late afternoon, just as the sun was slanting behind the tall oaks that surrounded the property in San Marino.

Sadia, Giovanni and Beatrice's human daughter, ran to the car as soon as it stopped. Chloe captured her in a hug as soon as the door opened.

"Ben told me your dad died." Sadia's voice trembled. "I'm sorry, Chloe. I'm sorry."

The girl's fierce embrace almost had Chloe crumpling again. "Thank you, Sadi." She kissed the girl's cheek. "I'm so glad I'm here now. I missed your hugs."

"I'll give you extra!" Sadia squeezed her arms around Chloe's neck. "Mama and I cleaned up your room. It's two doors from mine, and we picked flowers and put them in a vase for you."

"That is so kind. Thank you. I bet they're beautiful."

"They are. And Mr. Gavin is staying in the little house by the pool."

"So we'll see him when he wakes up."

Chloe walked with Sadia toward the house before she remembered her luggage. She turned and saw Audra and Zain grabbing her bags, along with a new security guard who had appeared with Audra that morning. "Can I get something?"

"Don't worry about it," the new guy said. "We'll get you settled."

"Thanks..."

He smiled. "Jeff."

"Jeff." She nodded. "Thanks."

She had no idea why Gavin felt the need to assign her extra security, and she usually didn't ask.

Should you?

Shouldn't his wife know?

Gavin's wife.

Sadia was talking, and Chloe wasn't paying attention. Luckily, she was pretty sure it was something about dance lessons because she ended with "Want to see me do it?"

Chloe nodded. "Absolutely. Where—?"

"Baba built me a whole room to practice my dancing!" Sadia ran into the house, taking off her shoes just beyond the french doors to the kitchen. "Dema, Chloe's here!"

Chloe saw Sadia's nanny rise and walk to the door, holding out her arms.

"My friend." Dema embraced her, strong arms holding Chloe up when her throat thickened with tears again. "I've been praying for you every day. How are you?"

Chloe cleared her throat and blinked back tears. "It's hard when things weren't good between us."

Dema loosened her embrace. "I know it must be." She frowned a little. "You're not drinking enough water; you look dehydrated. Why don't you go see the new studio and I'll bring you some tea."

Chloe forced a smile. "You and Gavin with the tea."

"But he brews you that fearful Scottish stew, and I made superior Syrian tea." She held up a hand. "It's fine. You don't have to tell him that mine is better." She smiled at Sadia. "You must show Chloe your dance room. She is a fellow dancer, so she will understand."

"It's so awesome." Sadia grabbed Chloe's hand, nearly knocking her over as she removed her shoes.

"I can't wait to see it." Chloe tried to forget her

sadness and focused on Sadia's bright energy. She followed the little girl through the familiar house that had been her refuge since she was fifteen.

Ben had been her first love, and his family had never allowed her to feel unwelcome, even after they broke up. They'd lost touch for about five years but reconnected when Ben moved to New York. His childhood home was far more familiar to her than her own.

The room Sadia led her to was once a home theater, but the deep couches had been removed, the walls had been mirrored on one side, and the windows were carefully angled to allow light in the room without direct sunlight.

"Mama comes and plays with me in here sometimes in the daytime."

"Oh, that's nice. Does she dance too?"

Sadia made a face that could only be described as patronizing. "Not as good as me, but she's getting better."

"I can't wait to see." Chloe managed not to laugh. "Okay, my best student, show me what you've learned."

She sat on one of the benches that lined the walls and watched as Sadia carefully picked a song from the computer in the corner and then positioned herself in front of the barre, facing the mirror.

The little girl was gifted, and it made Chloe's heart sing. Sadia adored dancing, and she would never know a time or a place where that wasn't celebrated. She would have the best instructors, attend the best classes, and receive flowers at every performance. She would never be faced with disappointed voices or pursed lips.

Chloe watched Sadia go through two routines, making gentle corrections if she saw the need, then stood and danced along when Sadia put on a video routine of kids hip-hop dancing she'd been learning on her own.

It was the balm Chloe's aching heart needed.

Hours must have passed, because when the final video ended, Chloe heard clapping from the doorway. She turned and saw Gavin standing in the doorway.

God, I love you.

He was dressed casually in a pair of faded jeans and a band T-shirt, his feet in socks.

"Incredible dancing, ladies." He pushed away from the door. "Sadia, you learn more every time I see you. I can see that you are practicing."

"Gavin!" Sadia skipped to him. "Do you know how to dance anything?" She grabbed his hands and bounced him toward the wooden dance floor.

He flashed a smile at the little girl. "I might know a few things that Chloe taught me."

He winked at Chloe, and her heart fell out of her chest and landed on the floor.

Again.

"What dance is it?" Sadia was jumping up and down. "I want to see."

"Cara," Chloe called to the computer system. "Play 'Ariele e Calibano' by Sineterra."

Gavin knew the music well. He walked toward her, his right arm held out. Chloe circled him as Sadia ran to the bench where Chloe had been sitting earlier. They met in the middle, and Gavin pulled Chloe into his chest as the music began to pick up pace.

The tango was the first dance she'd taught him, and he'd learned it to military precision like the perfectionist he was. After five years of dancing with her, he could lead

Chloe into a pitch-black room and dance the steps without missing a beat.

They moved effortlessly across the floor, her bare feet never even touching the edge of his feet; he was too careful to pinch a single toe.

She heard Sadia gasp as Gavin dipped her dramatically, pulled her close, then walked around her slowly in time with the music. She was trapped by his eyes; she could feel them on her body as he circled her. She heard him humming under his breath before he took her in his arms and they spun around the floor.

Chloe ignored the sudden twinge in her knee. It was familiar and nothing she hadn't danced through before. Less familiar was the painful realization that twisted in her chest.

He can dance this song forever, but you cannot.

You cannot.

Gavin sensed the change and quickly led them into a dramatic dip to finish the dance even though the music wasn't quite done.

"Wow!" Sadia clapped. "I want to learn that dance! Chloe, can you teach me that dance?"

"Of course."

Gavin locked his gaze with hers, unwilling to release her. "Good evening, dove."

"Good evening." She could barely catch her breath. Her back was arched and her arms outstretched.

He slowly pulled her upright, his eyes never leaving hers.

"I believe there's a conversation we didn't finish last night," he said quietly. "Why don't we find a quiet place to talk?"

7

_____

Gavin led her into the garden after bidding Sadia good night. The little girl was charming, but he needed Chloe to himself. He could tell she'd been stressed the entire day, and he cursed himself for his thoughtless outburst the night before.

"How was your day?" He kept her hand in his as he led them to a quiet sitting area behind the pool house.

Gavin didn't know what he'd been thinking except that after five years, Chloe was probably ready for a progression of their relationship. If she'd been with a human, she would expect that, wouldn't she? He wanted her to know he was committed to her.

She hadn't said a word since they stepped outside.

He led her to a chaise and sat across from her in a chair. "Please talk."

She took a deep breath. "You have never brought that up before. Not once. I didn't even know that you thought about..."

"Marriage?" He frowned. "I haven't thought about it. Not in a detailed way."

"So why did you bring it up?"

Now he was starting to worry. "Do you not want to get married?"

"I haven't thought about it any more than you."

"But I brought it up." He sat back and frowned. "And you didn't say yes."

"I didn't say no. You didn't actually ask me to marry you. You said, 'We should'—"

"Chloe, will you marry me?"

Her mouth fell open, and no sound escaped. Her eyes looked panicked, not thrilled.

The predator in Gavin rose to the surface. He stood and began to pace, considering his options. "You're not prepared to give me an answer?"

"I don't know what to say."

She loved him. He knew she loved him. But the more she hedged around answering his question, the more he wondered: Was there something she needed that he wasn't giving her? Was there something she wanted that he could not provide?

Chloe finally spoke. "This is something that just popped into your head, and I don't know what to tell you. We're together. We're happy. I just had a... huge shock."

He hadn't thought about that. Or maybe he had in the back of his mind. "You're saying it's not a good time."

"I'm saying... I'm asking why now? Why are you bringing this up now?"

Gavin shook his head. "I don't know."

Chloe had lost her father, and Gavin couldn't be with her during most of her mourning rituals. She was completely alone during the day, and he couldn't be there. Was he feeling insecure? Worrying that there were others who could provide her with comfort during times he could not? He'd smelled Zain on her as they danced. He knew the two were friends—knew Zain had his own romantic partner, in fact—but he also knew the human was attracted to Chloe and had been since he met her.

"Do you object to marriage?" Gavin stood with his hands clasped behind his back.

"As an institution? No."

"If you were with a human for five years, would you be thinking about marriage?"

Silence.

Gavin swung his head toward her when she said nothing. "Would you?"

"Probably." Her voice was small.

"But not when you're with a vampire."

Chloe stood. "I didn't think marriage was important to you! I didn't think about it because I am happy with who and what we are. That is enough for me. Is it enough for you?"

No.

Gavin caught the word before it erupted from his throat. "Why don't you want more?"

Chloe looked confused. "What more should I want? You're committed to me, right?"

"Of course I am."

"And I'm committed to you." She frowned. "I don't understand—"

"Where do you see us in five years?"

Chloe said nothing.

Gavin walked toward her. "In ten years? Twenty?"

Her expression finally cracked. "In twenty years, I'm going to be fifty." Her voice was small. Not timid but... small.

"And?" Gavin finally understood. "Do you think I'll be incapable of loving you when you're fifty?"

Tears welled in her eyes. "I'll be... not old, but older than you." She flexed her knee. "If I stay the way I am—"

"Your body won't stay the same." He kept his voice low. "Your knee will hurt you. Probably daily. The injury you had in your lower back two years ago might come back to haunt you. Your feet might need surgery one day; I've read on the subject."

"And if you marry me—"

"I will be committing myself to you for all of that." He put his hands on his hips. "Yes."

She swallowed hard and cleared her throat. "And beyond that, Gavin? When I'm my mother's age? Older?"

A knot of anger was growing in his chest.

"What about when I'm *really* old?" Chloe's voice rose. "What about when I start forgetting things? When I can barely move and—"

"Do you think my love has an *expiration date*?" He exploded, unable to stay silent any longer.

Her eyes went wide. "I'm not saying—"

"That is exactly what you are saying. Do you think so little of my regard for you? Do you think I am that shallow, Chloe? That I love only your beauty? Is that all you think I care about?" He could hear her heart pounding.

"No. But if I decide not to change, we are going to have to face reality, and if we marry—"

"That's what it is." Realization dawned. "You're leaving me an out. You're leaving *both* of us an out, is that it? We'll continue this relationship as long as it doesn't feel too uncomfortable for either of us, and then in twenty or thirty years if it doesn't suit you or me, we'll go our separate ways and be done with it, eh? No fuss and bother. No vows to break. No mess."

Her face was a careful mask. "I know you want me to change. You don't say it—you never bring it up—but I know you want—"

"Of course I fucking want you to change, Chloe!" He stepped back and ran a frustrated hand through his hair to keep himself from shaking. "I spent nearly two hundred years alone, and then I found you." He shook his head. "You charming, funny, magnetic, brilliant woman, of course I want you forever. But if I can't have you forever, don't fucking force me to cut short a minute of my time with you." He glared at her. "Don't push me away."

She was crying. Tears streamed down her cheeks, and she swiped the back of her hand over her face. "I don't know if I want kids. I kind of think right now that I don't, but what if I change my mind and—?"

"How many fucking vampire families do we know who have children, Chloe? Fucking hell, your group of friends is getting so bloody domestic it's like a morality play. How many children do Baojia and Natalie have now? Six? Ten? I half expect Ben and Tenzin to adopt something at the rate we're going."

Chloe sniffed and muttered, "Probably some terrible reptile I'll have to learn to feed."

She wasn't wrong. God help any human child that Ben and Tenzin tried to adopt.

He focused on Chloe. "Dove, you've been avoiding all these questions for five years now, and... I'm just as guilty of it."

She looked confused. "What do you mean?"

"What business was I in New Orleans to discuss? Why was I in Paris before that?"

She sat back on the chaise and used the edge of her shirt to wipe her eyes. "Gavin, it's none of my business what you're—"

"No, but see, it is. It should be. If you were with a human, you would know what he did for work." He walked toward her and took her hand, getting down on one knee in front of her. "Ninety-nine percent of the vampire world doesn't even know you exist. I did that partly to protect you and partly to protect myself. I was... afraid to scare you off. If we marry—"

"We don't have to—"

"*If we marry*" —he gentled his voice— "it will mean we are binding ourselves together whether you decide to change or not. You would have to accept more of my world."

She stared at the ground, and her normally expressive face was a mask. "Would that be riskier than what we have now?"

He took a breath. "At this point, it would actually be safer for you to be known as my wife than as my human lover."

"I don't understand."

"Lovers come and go. Mates, husbands, wives, they have... status. Socially and financially, you would be seen as my partner in the immortal world, so the allies I have cultivated over the years would be forced to extend that relationship to you as well."

She nodded slowly. "Got it."

"But that is not why I want to marry you."

She looked up. "Why do you want to marry me?"

"Because I'm a selfish bastard and I never want anyone else to put his bloody hands on you for the rest of your life; you're mine."

She blinked. "Well... that's honest."

"I *love* you for all the reasons previously stated. You're brilliant, kind, funny, and make me enjoy being a living fossil. But I want to *marry* you because I'm a bloody selfish bastard."

"And to keep me safer."

"And that. But no matter what you choose, know that I *will* keep you safe." He leaned forward and captured her lips with his own. He allowed himself to be enveloped in her scent, let his amnis flood over her skin. He wanted to surround her, consume her.

Be consumed.

And yet he needed to say the rest. He needed to give her the knot of words that threatened to choke him.

"Never doubt that I love you with every fiber of my being," Gavin said as he pulled away. "But you need to make some decisions, Chloe. Deciding to be with me *or not* is about more than just children or aging or any of that. It's about living your life."

"What are you talking about?"

"Right now you have a life in the human world. Or you could. You could leave me" —his fangs ached in his jaw, threatening to erupt— "marry a human, and have a normal life. Have a normal family."

"Gavin, I don't—"

"If you haven't thought about it, you need to." He stood carefully. "You need to at least consider it, or you will always harbor doubts."

She narrowed her eyes. "So I should marry you, but before I do, I should think about leaving you and marrying a random human I've never met?"

"You need to think about the future you want, whether it involves me or not."

She stood and huffed out a breath. "Are you serious?"

"Of course I am."

She stared at him, then started walking away. "Stupid vampires and their stupid—" She spun around. "You know, maybe I should go on a few experimental dates with some humans while I'm in California. Maybe just try a couple of guys out, see what I think?"

He bared his teeth and felt his feet leave the ground.

"Yeah." She crossed her arms. "That's what I thought." Chloe rolled her eyes and continued walking toward the house.

～

GAVIN TAPPED a pen on a yellow legal pad. "I was trying to be... moderate. Reasonable."

Audra raised an eyebrow. "Boss, you proposed and then basically told her to second-guess everything you were saying and to consider leaving you and having a life with a human."

"It's a future she could have if she wants it." He shuffled the stack of papers Audra handed him.

Gavin and his security team were meeting with Audra in one of the Vecchio cottages near the pool. It didn't have an office, but they were using the table to lay out their schedule for the upcoming week. He had planned on taking this meeting in the office of his largest club, but Chloe wasn't speaking to him at the moment and he didn't want to pull Audra from Chloe, so he'd called everyone to San Marino.

"She could have a normal life," Gavin repeated. "And she needs to consider that carefully."

Audra squinted. "Does she though?"

His chief of security for the Los Angeles properties poured from a bottle of heated blood-wine and passed him a glass. "It's not easy to meet people." Raj was a fairly young vampire Gavin had poached from a Singaporean rival. "I mean, I've only been a vampire for about ten years, but I don't think dating has gotten any easier."

Semis, his new day man, nodded understandingly. "It's not simple out there, boss. I envy you and Chloe."

Raj nodded. "I think we all do."

Audra said, "I think if anything ever happened to Gary, I would just stay single for the rest of my life. I'm forty-two; I can't online date. It would be a disaster."

Semis sighed. "Online dating is rough, man. I can't meet *anyone* in New York."

Raj nodded. "It's not easier in LA. All the nice women I know are married with married friends or lesbians with lesbian friends."

Semis pointed at him. "Truth."

Gavin glared at them all. "Can we focus please?"

All three of them looked down at the detailed schedule Audra had printed out.

"Dr. Reardon's memorial service is on Wednesday at ten in the morning," Audra said. "The viewing is the night before. Gavin, you will be going to that, correct?"

"Yes. It's in the evening, so I can attend. Obviously I can't attend the funeral. Semis, I'd like you and Audra to both be there for Chloe. I know Dema will also be attending."

Semis nodded. "You got it, boss."

Audra continued, "So far, activity around the Reardon house is minimal. Chloe says she wants to stay here, so that simplifies things a lot because we can piggyback off the Vecchios' security."

"Has there been additional activity?" Gavin asked.

"You're in town, but you're not in the usual haunts," Raj said. "You and Chloe *have* attracted some attention."

"Raj and his people are tracking two groups that seem to be watching her," Audra said. "One, we're pretty sure, is made up of Ernesto's people. You might want to talk to Beatrice."

Gavin nodded. "She's not my biggest fan, but she'll call her grandfather and tell him to call off his dogs for Chloe. The other group?"

"We're not sure yet, but they could be French," Raj said. "One of my guys says he thinks they were speaking French, but at least one of them is African."

"Lots of Africans speak French," Gavin muttered. "Could be Vivian being a pest."

"Does she know about Chloe?"

"Yes, but minimally. She might be trying to gather information. I'll reach out." Gavin's sister was his own personal pain in the arse, and she didn't need to be stalking Chloe to gather information for her schemes.

He looked at Semis. "Anything else?"

"You got two emails from Marie-Hélène," Semis said. "An email from Lagos about a new liquor distributor. I think the manager just wants to double-check with you on the deal. Some other minor stuff, but that's about it."

"And I talked with Veronica this morning," Audra said. "I think she emailed you a report too. Everything in New York is set for you to spend the rest of the week out here if you need to, and Pete is happy and hasn't torn up her new couch yet."

"Excellent." The last thing he needed was Veronica to stop cat-sitting for him and Chloe because Pete couldn't control his attraction to upholstery.

In the past, Gavin had preferred to keep his team loose and decentralized, but his organization had been growing over the past six years and would grow even more with the new technology project with Marie-Hélène.

He was going to have to hire more people.

"Raj, do you still have contacts in Singapore?"

The young vampire raised an eyebrow. "A few. I didn't burn any major bridges."

"I think I'm going to be looking for at least two new people in the next six months—a security coordinator in New Orleans who'll be flexible about working with Marie-Hélène's people and a day guard here. If Chloe agrees to marry me, her mother becomes a target."

Raj nodded. "Got it. I'll see who might be looking to make a move."

"I might know someone in Hong Kong who would be good for Chloe's mom," Semis said. "Want me to email her?"

"A woman would probably be ideal." Gavin nodded. "We just need to be prepared."

Just in case.

Usually Gavin could predict his lover's actions quite well, but Chloe was annoyed with him, grieving her father, and he'd thrown a series of life-altering questions at her with little plan for the fallout.

Fine, she was annoyed at him for a good reason.

Gavin stood and straightened his shirt. "Run along and do the things you do, children. I'm going to try to find Chloe. She'll want to know about Pete."

"Sure," Audra whispered. "She needs to know about the *cat*."

Gavin glared at her. "Don't you have work?"

Audra, ever his tormenter, turned to Semis. "He's

checking up on her to make sure she hasn't signed up for any dating apps."

Semis looked at Gavin. "Tell her to avoid Tinder; it will suck out her soul."

Raj muffled a laugh.

Gavin's eyes swept the table of unhelpful employees. "I sign your paychecks. Remember that."

"Yes, boss."

"Of course you do." Audra rose to accompany him. "I should get back to Chloe."

Raj thumped a fist over his heart. "All the love, Gavin."

Gavin was tempted to bite one of them, but there was only one person he really wanted to bite, and she wasn't speaking to him.

He turned to Audra as they walked toward the door. "What the hell is Tinder?"

"You don't want to know."

8

———

Chloe sat through her father's homegoing service beside her mother, listening to the pastor regale them with stories of her father's life, his work, his activism, and a faith that she'd never seen the soft hand of in her life.

But John Washington Reardon had been born the son of an eminent pastor and so a rousing and lively celebration of his life was surely to be expected. There was a full gospel choir in purple satin robes, oceans of white flowers, and tearful reflections from his colleagues, his patients, and his peers.

Her name was mentioned a few times, but the main thrust of the service was to honor a father who had seemed to give his absolute heart and soul to everyone other than his family.

A woman in a soft grey dress and net-covered hat stood behind the podium, dabbing at tears and fighting to read the paper in front of her.

"When Dr. Reardon found out that my father had been laid off and we no longer had health insurance, he pushed to get me into an experimental study that would be fully paid. He called, he filled out forms. I can't even imagine everything he did for me. And even when he wasn't my doctor, he called the specialists who were taking care of me, letting them know that I was..." She sniffed and gathered her strength. "...a *special* patient. He treated me like family, and I can't..." She looked up and found Chloe's mother. "I don't think I would be alive today without him. I wouldn't have my two beautiful children or my husband. My parents would have lost their only child." She blinked back tears. "Dr. Reardon was truly one of the best men I have ever known, and he will be so missed." She folded the paper. "So missed. Thank you for letting me pay my respects."

Clara nodded graciously, a demure smile on her face, while Chloe sat next to her, frozen by a stranger's memories of a man she'd never known.

Was that why her father had always been so distant to her? Was he saving his devotion and affection for his patients? And if so, wasn't she the selfish one? Were her needs more important than theirs? She'd never experienced juvenile cancer. She'd never fought for her life. What was her lonely childhood to the holy mission of medicine her father had pursued?

Patient after patient, grateful parents and grandparents. The service went on for three hours while her father's life and work were celebrated. Chloe felt like she was drifting through the day on autopilot—standing in a receiving line, receiving greetings and unwelcome hugs from relatives she hadn't seen in a decade.

The graveside ceremony was a true sham. There was no casket because her father had long ago signed papers to donate his body to science—his last noble gesture—which meant all Chloe and her relatives were doing was dedicating a place where her father's cremated remains would eventually be put in the ground after medical students were done with him.

It all felt hollow, empty like the hole in the ground that hadn't even been dug. Chloe ached for something solid. She wanted to hear the thunk of a casket being lowered. She wanted to see her father's face, even if it was in death. She wanted to put a gardenia on his casket and touch... something.

But there was nothing. Memories from other people who knew and missed her father in a way she never could.

If she followed Gavin into immortality, this grief would be played out over and over again. She would slowly watch everyone she had ever known in life die before her. Her mother, of course. Her aunts. Her cousins and the babies that followed their every step.

Her friends.

Arthur and Drew. Zain. Dema. Audra. All her friends from the dance company.

They would all be gone, and she would feel this hollow ache in her chest over and over and over.

Just like Gavin would if you remain human.

Except it would be worse. So much worse. To stay with her, watch her decay. Or lose her to a car crash or a heart attack like her father.

"Do you think my love has an expiration date?"

She was very afraid that it didn't. After five years of life with the man, she'd seen his dark side, seen the creeping depression that he battled to contain at times. She'd watched him fight back his most selfish instincts to give her the kindness and stability she needed.

She'd also seen the edge of violence and his fierce

loyalty to the few people he counted as friends. He had employees and people he looked after, but the people Gavin truly cared about? She could count them on her fingers.

"I spent nearly two hundred years alone, and then I found you."

She couldn't think about that now. She didn't want to think about it at all, but especially not when she was standing at the future gravesite of a father she had never known, the man she'd spent her adult life disappointing.

She was tired and she wanted Gavin, but it would be hours before he woke. Hours of shallow pleasantries at her mother's house. Hours entertaining family who judged her and asked in quiet tones why her "boyfriend" wasn't there.

I don't care.

She could tell herself that over and over, but she did.

Audra touched the back of her arm, startling her out of her reverie in the graveyard. "You ready?"

Chloe blinked and looked around, realizing that everyone was walking back to the cars without her. Dema was waiting at a polite distance.

"Where're Semis and Zain?" She frowned, looking for the men.

"They went to start the car." Audra nodded toward the long line of luxury cars that was winding out of the cemetery. "Come on. Just a few more hours."

Until Gavin was awake and she felt something solid again.

Chloe nodded and walked over the uneven grass. Dema hooked her arm through Chloe's as they walked.

"I'm so sorry, Chloe." Dema kept her voice low. "I can't imagine—"

"I'm fine." Her voice was wooden. "I didn't really know him, I guess. All these people lost a brother, a friend, a beloved doctor." She glanced over her shoulder. "I lost a stranger."

SHE COUNTED the hours until sundown, sitting in the shade of the backyard to escape the oppressive scent of gardenias in the house. They were her father's favorite. Neat, glossy green leaves with fragrant pure white blossoms. Gardenias were perfect hothouse flowers that took well to formal gardens and bloomed through the summer.

When she was a teenager, she'd looked up the meaning of the flower. It was a bloom sent to signal secret or unexpressed love. It also had a lot of generic meanings like familial love, purity, and friendship.

If her father had been sentimental, Chloe might have read some meaning into a reserved man having the gardenia as a favorite flower, but her mother told her years later that Grandmother Reardon had won multiple prizes for her gardenias when her father was growing up in Georgia. So Chloe figured gardenias probably symbolized winning for her father.

Which fit better than unexpressed love.

Her parents' garden was a formal arrangement with a gazebo marking the end of a lush lawn that ran from the back sitting area past the rectangular pool and on through an alley of crepe myrtles and agapanthus that nodded their bright purple heads as she walked by.

Zain was sitting in the gazebo when she found him, playing something on his phone.

"Hey you." He patted the seat next to his, staring at

the house. "This is the most Southern house and garden I've ever seen in LA."

She sat and leaned back against the wooden railing. "Yeah, they did their best to re-create their childhoods, didn't they?"

"Uh-huh." He looked down at her. "You tired of the mourners yet?"

"I was tired of them days ago." She watched the late-afternoon sun hit the pure white siding of the colonial house. "Who's driving Gavin over?"

Zain frowned. "It's just him; he'll fly."

"Right." She took a deep breath. "Do you think we can leave for New York tomorrow? Or tonight?"

His eyebrows went up. "You that ready to leave LA, huh?"

"I'm tired of all this." She waved a hand in front of the house. "My mother, her sisters, my dad's family. I don't know any of them anymore. They're all doctors and lawyers and... well, Keisha does something with robotics programing in Boston—I have no idea what any of that is. All my cousins are married or engaged or having babies with their spouses. There are four children under five in that house, and I don't know any of their names."

Zain chuckled, then looked at Chloe's face. "You feeling some kind of way about that?"

"I don't know them," she said. "And they treat me like some kind of oddity. 'You still doing that dancing thing?' A few of them asked if I was in a Broadway show and then laughed when I told them I just performed at Lincoln Center."

"That show was incredible. We caught the livestream the night of the premier."

"It was great, right?" She laughed. "And they don't

care. At all. I could be stripping and they'd probably see it about the same way."

"Those girls do put the work in though."

She smiled. "You'd never catch me arguing."

Zain put his arm around Chloe's shoulders and they sat in silence, watching the sun drop lower over the manicured backyard.

He squeezed her shoulders. "Just because they're blood doesn't mean they're family."

"I know that." She sighed. "But they are."

"Your mom falling apart without her daughter at her side?"

"No, she was fine as soon as Aunt Sheila got here."

"So..." Zain shrugged. "Go home. Throw a few pints back at the Dancing Bear, go shopping with your weird fashion friend—"

"Arthur isn't weird; he's gifted."

"He wanted to dye my dreadlocks pink."

Chloe couldn't stop her laugh. "I mean... Okay, I'd forgotten about that, but he's really very normal in other ways, I promise."

"He and Tenzin buddies?"

"As much as she is with any human who doesn't know about vampires."

"Then I rest my case." He squeezed her shoulder one more time and let her go. "I love seeing you, but when my grandpa died, all I wanted was to be home. So go home. Be with *your* people, not your mom's. Mourn in whatever way you need to mourn." Zain looked at the house. "They're not... maybe they never have been your people. They definitely aren't anymore."

She opened her mouth, but he stopped her.

"Mourn whatever you need to mourn," he added.

"Yes, your father's death. But you're allowed to mourn for the relationship you didn't have too. Mourn the father he wasn't that you wanted him to be. You get to grieve for all that, Chloe. Mourn for it, because you deserved to have it."

Chloe took a deep breath and nodded. "Mourn the life I thought I'd have that didn't happen."

"And celebrate the life you do have," Zain said. "Even if it's not what you imagined."

She nodded. "I don't want to go back. Not to any of this. My future isn't here."

Her future was with a dark lover who treasured her, who had never neglected or abandoned her. A man who understood what it meant to be alone and cherished her even more because of it.

"I think I'm going to marry Gavin," Chloe said.

Zain's eyebrows went up. "I have all kind of questions, but maybe put your game face back on for now because your mother is walking out here."

"Right." Chloe stood and walked out of the gazebo. "Hey, Mom."

"Getting some fresh air?" Clara was dressed in an impeccable dove-grey suit and a navy hat. "Your cousins are all inside. Brother Archibald just left, and they were going to put on a movie for the little ones." She looked around Chloe. "I thought maybe Gavin had arrived. I heard you talking."

"No, he'll be here around seven." She frowned. "I was just talking with Zain."

"Your friend with the long hair?" Clara frowned. "I didn't see him go in the house."

Chloe smiled. "What are you talking about?" She turned. "He's right..."

Zain was nowhere in the backyard.

Chloe's eyes swept the grounds, taking in the heavy brush along the property lines and the expansive lawn. Zain hadn't walked past them and he wasn't visible.

She gripped her mother's shoulder. "Mom, go to the house and get Audra."

"What—?"

"Right now, Mom!"

Her mother turned and walked quickly when she heard the urgency in Chloe's voice.

Chloe stayed on the walkway, scanning her surroundings. She was visible from the house, and she was counting on that giving her some security.

"Zain?"

It was probably nothing. He'd probably slipped out the side yard or he was checking with the security team along the back fence.

"Zain!"

She got her phone out and texted him.

Where RU?

She heard a faint chime from the bushes and a rustling sound.

Fuck.

Chloe turned and started to run toward the house, but the pinching pain in her neck told her it was too late.

The darkness took her.

9

Gavin woke and knew something was wrong. He could smell humans and vampires waiting outside his day chamber. He checked his phone and saw three messages from Chloe, all in the last three hours before he woke.

No greeting from his lover when he woke and four vampires and a human waiting outside his chamber.

Fear manifested in his belly, chilling his heart and cooling his blood. He carefully dressed in the pair of black combat pants he always packed, pulled on a black T-shirt and boots before he opened the door.

He stared at the eyes watching him. Giovanni Vecchio, Raj, Ben, Tenzin, and Audra.

"Tell me."

"Chloe was taken from the back garden at her mother's house." Audra's face was washed of color and her eyes looked dead. "They shot a tranquilizer dart at Zain, and we think they probably did the same to Chloe. Her mother ran in the house to get me, but when I reached the backyard, they were already gone."

His mind began to slot pieces of information into a framework. He ignored the raging fear and the temptation to take Audra's head off. Rage would not find Chloe. Anger would not find her. Cold, clinical deduction was his only weapon.

Before dusk, not vampires.

Tranquilizer, not silenced firearm.

"Boss, I'm sorry. I thought we had her—"

"Quiet." Gavin cut her off. "I don't want to hear from you unless you know where Chloe is."

Audra shook her head.

"Then be quiet." Gavin's mind was turning over scenarios. "She's alive, and they want something from me," he said quietly. "They've taken her as leverage." He looked at Ben. "What do you know?"

Giovanni stepped forward. "Come up to the library. Beatrice has been on the phone with her grandfather's people." The fire vampire led them out of the guesthouse, across the lawn, and toward the main house. "Whether they realize it or not, by attacking Zain, they've violated Ernesto's aegis since Zain works for Beatrice and she's under Ernesto's protection."

"Zain will be fine," Ben said. "He's feeling pretty sick, but there were no lasting—"

"I don't care about Zain." The human hadn't been strong enough to protect Chloe, and that was all he cared about. "Chloe is smaller than Zain; if they used the same dosage on her, it could be highly damaging."

He looked at Tenzin, whose eyes were as cold or colder than his. "Are you with me?"

"Wherever you need to go," she said quietly.

Gavin knew if there was one vampire he could depend on to do *whatever* was required to get Chloe back, it was Tenzin. She would do the necessary thing even if others hesitated.

"Every vampire in Los Angeles will be looking for them," Ben said. "We've already told Ernesto that Chloe is yours."

Not enough.

Gavin allowed himself a moment of anger, cursing himself for hiding their connection. If he'd been more open about who Chloe was to him, only a vampire with a death wish would have touched her. Whoever it was had banned him or herself from sanctuary around the world.

He glanced at Audra, then to Raj, his head of security. "Her mother?"

"Safe," Raj offered. "We've put additional guards on the house and circling the neighborhood. I managed to keep her mother from filing a police report, but that's only going to hold her off for a few hours unless we get her back."

They entered the house and headed straight for the upstairs library, where he could already hear Beatrice De Novo speaking with someone in rapid Spanish. As they entered the room, she caught Gavin's eye and nodded.

"I have to go," she said to whomever was on the phone. "When I get more information, I'll contact you."

The voice on the phone responded. "We'll email the list now."

She turned to Gavin. "Ernesto's chief of security is emailing a list of every visiting party in his territory that has asked permission to be here. Obviously, there's no guarantee—"

"This is probably an unauthorized party." Gavin knew that if kidnapping Chloe was the goal, it was far more likely that whoever had taken her had *not* asked formal permission to operate in Ernesto's territory, which meant they were rogues and he could kill them. "It had to be someone who knew who she was to me. There would be no point in taking her otherwise."

"Unless they were targeting me." Tenzin's voice was soft.

Gavin's eyes swung toward her. "Explain."

"She wasn't working on anything dangerous; I would have told you and Audra," Tenzin said. "But she's my personal assistant. She has access to large amounts of money and private information for both Ben and me."

"Have you checked your accounts?"

"As soon as I heard. Nothing stands out, but..." Tenzin shrugged. "It could have been either of us."

"If I'd been open about our relationship, she wouldn't have been taken."

Raj said, "Boss, you don't know that."

Gavin glared at him. "Have any of our other human employees been targeted?"

Raj sighed. "No one would dare."

"Exactly."

Giovanni spoke loudly. "Blame is pointless right now. We need to find her." He turned to Beatrice. "Where are we on traffic cameras and other surveillance footage?"

Beatrice turned to a wall of monitors that had been mounted next to a row of bookcases. "Cara, display on."

The monitors all came to life, showing a series of what looked like low-resolution security-camera footage from low angles. Addresses crawled across the bottom of each screen in dull white letters.

"I hacked into the most common security system used in the area and found dozens of doorbell cameras in that neighborhood. Their firewalls are ridiculous."

Cars slipped along the residential streets joined by the occasional pedestrian, half a dozen cats, and a stray dog. A few bicycles were visible going from one frame to the next.

"This camera" —Beatrice pointed to the top right corner— "is directly across the street from the house that backs up to the Reardons'. They didn't go out the front, so if they had Chloe tranquilized and needed to get her into a car, they would have gone through the back of one of these houses on the street north of the Reardons'. Probably had a van waiting."

"A van would stand out," Gavin muttered. "In that neighborhood, you wouldn't see a van unless it looked like a work truck. She's tranquilized, they could have put her in any vehicle and she would look like she was sleeping."

"Good point," Beatrice said. "Cara, rewind footage to start at three thirty this afternoon."

Gavin kept his eyes trained on the corner monitor. A few cars drove by, but none stopped.

"Cara, forward at two times speed," Beatrice said. "Cara, stop!"

A dark SUV pulled up to the house just before four o'clock, and two figures slipped out. Both were male, one was white and the other black. They were wearing casual dress clothes that looked like European labels with thick-soled black combat boots. The white man had a messenger bag slung over his shoulder.

Raj sidled up to Gavin. "The French speakers?"

"Possibly."

"I can't tell what kind of car that is," Ben said.

"Range Rover, maybe?" Raj offered. "Land Cruiser. Could be a lower-end model too. Can't read the plate."

Beatrice spoke again. "Cara, forward at two times

speed."

Gavin spotted movement just before five o'clock. "Cara, stop!"

The two men had returned, carrying Chloe between them. To anyone walking by, they would have looked like two men supporting an injured woman. They opened the back door of the SUV and carefully placed her inside.

"Did they put a seat belt on her?" Raj narrowed his eyes. "They were careful, boss. They didn't want her hurt."

"Remind me to thank them when we meet." Gavin kept his eyes trained on the monitors, watching as the SUV pulled away. "There!" He pointed to the middle monitor on the bottom row. "It shows up there next."

Ben was standing over a map. "Got the address. It's two blocks from the first location, going west."

Tenzin walked over to the map, grabbed Ben's marker, and quickly drew dots in front of three more locations. "The vehicle headed west, then north."

Ben sighed. "Right for the 210 freeway. They could be anywhere."

"Have the list from Ernesto's people." Audra walked over, carrying a stack of papers. "They copied me and Raj too." She handed one to Raj and one to Gavin.

Raj scanned the list, shaking his head. "I don't recognize any—"

"I do." Gavin spotted her name immediately, and his fangs dropped. "Not French, Belgian." He was already walking toward the french doors that led to the backyard balcony. "Tenzin?"

"We're with you." Tenzin and Ben followed him, taking to the air a second behind him.

Gavin was hunting now.

~

SHE CLOSED her eyes and sighed. "I don't know how many times I can tell you: I have no idea what you're talking about. I am not... some top secret new employee. And I don't know anything about Gavin's businesses. I am a *bartender*."

"Haven't we treated you well?" The elegant man sitting across from her was human, like her. Black like her, though he spoke with an elegant French accent. "How is your headache, Miss Reardon?"

"My headache is fine." She stood and paced around the small room. "Listen, none of your questions make sense. I am not telling stories. I'm not trying to hide who I am."

Which was a lie.

"We know you are employed by Wallace's organization. We wish you no harm, Miss Reardon, I promise. Think of this as an opportunity."

"An opportunity?" She leaned on the table. "I am a bartender at the Dancing Bear in Brooklyn. I'm not special. I don't know any secrets."

Except the ones his girlfriend would know, but Chloe was pretty sure it was safer to go with the bartender story, and no one needed to know about Gavin's collection of plaid underwear but her.

"We are not trying to intimidate you, Miss Reardon, but—"

"You're not trying to intimidate me?" she yelled. "You kidnapped me from my mother's house on the day of my father's funeral!"

"After you expressed that you would be leaving Los

Angeles far sooner than my employer anticipated," the man said. "Truly, all this unpleasantness—"

"What's going to be unpleasant" —Chloe's eyes went wide— "is when Gavin finds you. Because he will, and it is not going to go well for you. You need to let me go. Blindfold me and drop me off in the middle of nowhere with a burner phone if you want to stay alive. I promise I am shit at describing people, so you're safe on that front, but if he finds me here and you're still holding me—"

"But why would an important immortal like Gavin Wallace care so much about a simple bartender, Miss Reardon?" The man's eyebrow rose. "If you are what you say you are, why does he have so many of his people guarding you?"

Fuck.

She tried another tack and sat across the table from the man. She was being held in a small room with a bed, a sofa, a small dining table, and a private bathroom with no windows. It was far nicer than her first apartment in Queens, and if she hadn't remembered the pinching pain in her neck and waking up with strangers, she could have fooled herself she was in a very generic hotel room or studio apartment.

"Listen, Mr....?"

"You may call me Mr. Chopel."

"Mr. Chopel, I am a bartender, but I'm also a friend. My father passed away and Gavin knew I was upset, so he sent Audra with me. Zain isn't even Gavin's employee —he's just a friend in Los Angeles who works for a family friend of mine, Giovanni Vecchio."

The man's pleasant gaze faltered. "The man guarding you...?"

"He wasn't a guard, he's a friend of mine, and yes, he

works for the Vecchio clan." Chloe could tell she'd thrown them off. "For your sake, I really hope Zain is okay."

Mr. Chopel turned to the thin man in the corner with the ascetic face and said something in a language that reminded Chloe of French but wasn't. She'd taken more than two years of French, but it had been a while since she practiced.

The man in the corner was human as well, white, with narrow lips and thinning sandy-brown hair. He hadn't said a word since Chloe had woken up. Now he answered the man in a low voice in a language that sounded more German than French.

What the hell?

"We're not going to talk about Giovanni Vecchio right now," the man questioning her said. "Tell us about the telecommunications project. Tell us about your programming work. Whatever he is paying you, our employer will pay double."

Chloe slowly banged her head on the table. "I am not a programmer. I don't know anything about technology. I am a bartender and a ballet dancer."

"Ballet?" The man laughed. "What use would Gavin Wallace have to hire a ballet dancer?"

"You don't believe me?" She toed off her sandals and kicked her right foot up and onto the table. "Do you see this?"

Both men visibly cringed.

"Ugly, right? I just got finished with a series of performances where I had to be in pointe shoes a lot. It was really hard on my feet, and I have the blisters and calluses to prove it. Do these look like the feet of someone who sits behind a desk and programs all day?"

The men exchanged glances, and she could see doubt

beginning to bloom.

"I do not know what information you have been given, but—"

"Word has gotten out, Miss Reardon. People know about Wallace's takeover of the immortal communications business. We know about his venture with Charmont Industries; they are already buying up space and advertising for experienced programmers. But you" —he pointed at her— "are the only one he hired away from a lab with security clearances from the Pentagon, so we know you must be the key."

Chloe's eyes went wide. "What are you talking about?"

"Your PhD dissertation—"

"I don't have a PhD—I never even went to college!"

"—was on voice command in robotic programming, so the implications for vampire technology are obvious. You must understand." He leaned on the table and smiled broadly. "My employer is very generous, Miss Reardon. *Name your price.* This is not a kidnapping, this is a job offer."

What kind of batshit-crazy vampire kidnapped people for job interviews?

Okay, never mind. Chloe could probably think of three off the top of her head who might think that was a great idea.

The man continued. "Mr. Wallace must have offered you a substantial sum if you left your lab in Boston, but I promise you, my employer's coffers are even deeper than his and you would have your pick of locations. There would be no demand that you..." He chuckled a little. "... uproot your life to live among the alligators."

"Oh my God." Chloe felt like she was in an alternate

universe. "Boston? I don't even..."

She blinked and part of the puzzle fell into place.

Boston.

Robotics programming.

They thought Chloe was her cousin Keisha.

Oh my God, they thought she was a brilliant computer programmer.

Fuck.

But alligators?

New Orleans.

They must have been digging into Gavin's new project—which had to be what he was in New Orleans to negotiate with Marie-Hélène—and looked up her last name and found her cousin Keisha's published work.

Fuck.

The last thing she wanted was for whoever this vampire was to go after her cousin Keisha who was happily programming robots for medical technology or something like that and engaged to be married to a botanist next year.

Then again, she didn't want them to murder her when they figured out she had no fucking clue what they were talking about and she was simply a very dangerous liability they were hiding.

She needed to kill time. Enough time for Gavin to find her. They were in LA, which meant that Gavin not only had all of his own people but Ben, Tenzin, and all the Vecchios.

If Chloe could distract her captors long enough, Gavin would find her.

She had to believe that.

She swallowed the lump in her throat and folded her hands on the table. "You said I could name my price?"

10

G avin hovered over the nondescript office building in Irvine. In the past three hours, he'd identified Chloe's exact location by tracking the humans Mila Anker had brought with her, the two men Raj had already identified watching Chloe.

Mila was Belgian, not French, but he kicked himself for not seeing the connection earlier.

The men who had taken Chloe were two of Mila's humans. Paul Chopel, a Congolese-Belgian lieutenant in the Anker organization Mila had inherited when her sire Rens was killed in London years before. And Luc De Smet, a Flemish marksman who had a reputation Gavin was ready to end on sight.

The men who'd taken Chloe were dangerous even if they were human. One didn't last in the Anker organization if they weren't willing to get blood on their hands, and no one hired a marksman for his intellect.

There were only a few floating scraps of information about De Smet and none about Chopel, but one tidbit was that the Flemish man was an avid follower of the Belgian football club Mechelen, who'd had a match with their rivals the previous weekend.

Gavin knew the owner of every sports bar in Los Angeles that regularly played European football games because it was his business to know, and only one of them would pay to play Belgian matches when they had such a small audience. A personal visit to the bar had netted the make, model, and plate numbers of the car Chopel and De Smet were driving in Los Angeles, a dark green Toyota Land Cruiser with black California plates that matched the model of the car they'd seen on the security footage.

Another call from Beatrice to Ernesto unearthed the discreet agency that had handled the rental for Mila's people, and another hack into their online security system gave Gavin the current GPS coordinates.

"She was stupid to register with Ernesto," Ben said, watching as vampires and humans milled in front of the office building. "He's arresting her tonight at a reception he invited her to and she happily accepted. As if she hadn't attacked someone in his own granddaughter's household."

"As if we couldn't find her trail," Gavin muttered.

"It wasn't stupid; it was arrogant," Tenzin said.

"When is the reception?" They needed to wait for Mila to be taken, but they also had to be sure she didn't get a message to the men holding Chloe.

Ben pulled out a phone in a thick, awkward case and shook it to activate the screen and check the time. "Fifteen minutes ago. Beatrice said she'd text when Ernesto took her into the meeting."

Ostensibly, Mila Anker was an up-and-coming information merchant trying to revive the organization left by her sire and his brother after they'd been killed, but Gavin knew the truth because he'd once considered Mila... if not a friend, then a friendly peer. She'd already been quietly trading information to the highest bidder for years, and she was extremely wealthy.

Mila Anker was like Gavin—no alliances, no loyalties. She was hired to find information discreetly, and she was very good at what she did. She was also known as a neutral player who didn't pass judgment on her clients, which was why Gavin had approached her with the telecom proposal months before. Though he'd ultimately changed his mind and told Mila he was rethinking the idea, he'd believed they were parting on good terms.

What he was really rethinking was Mila. Beneath all shining veneers, she was a spy, and nobody trusted spies.

Now she'd kidnapped Chloe and put a tranquilizer dart in one of Beatrice De Novo's people, which meant Mila was dead. If Beatrice didn't kill her, Ernesto would for violating the terms of her visit in his territory.

"The minute Mila's people know she's dead, they'll be in survival mode. They'll try to get rid of any evidence they were here and scatter," Gavin said.

Ben nodded. "We need to be ready to move."

"Ernesto's people will already be on the road," Tenzin said. "We should go in now."

"We wait for the text." Gavin kept his eyes on the building. "Or we wait for—"

Movement.

It was a young vampire with dark curly hair and a nearly milk-white complexion. He froze for a second; then his knees gave way.

"Now," Gavin yelled. "He's her child!"

Mila had brought one of her vampire children with her, and the minute a child's sire was dead, their immortal connection would be severed.

Dammit. Something must have gone wrong at Ernesto's.

Gavin, Ben, and Tenzin dove toward the office building, swords drawn. Every one of their targets knew their boss was dead, and only a severed head would kill a vampire. Mila's people were cornered animals.

Tenzin landed first, going directly for the black-haired vampire on his knees who was already drawing a weapon. Foolish immortal—it was only a gun.

Tenzin lifted a curved silver blade and slashed from the back of the man's neck to the front. His head dropped to the asphalt with a thunk. Ben landed behind her, a black-clad angel of death moving so quickly that three vampires dropped to the ground almost as one, their necks twisted at an unholy angle while the humans around them shouted in confusion.

Those shouts propelled Gavin through the glass doors of the office building, which shattered with a bloody punch. He landed in the shard-strewn foyer and took a deep breath, scenting for his mate.

There.

Her blood was spiked with acrid adrenaline, feeding the cold rage in Gavin's belly. He flew down the hallway, breaking down the door that divided Chloe from his protection.

A large man waited on the other side of the door, a handgun pointing at him.

Paul Chopel.

He screamed, "Don't come any closer or she's dead!"

Gavin looped a gust of wind behind the man, making him stumble forward into his grasp. He twisted his neck, feeling the pop of the man's spine breaking under his fingers, grabbed the gun from the human's limp hand, and pointed it at De Smet, who already had a small revolver pointed at Chloe's temple and his hand over her mouth.

"Hello, dove," Gavin said softly. "Give me a few more moments and we'll have you out of here."

She was shivering, and he could see that she was crying, but Gavin kept his eyes on De Smet.

"You're an independent operator, and your client is dead," Gavin said steadily. "If you let her go and leave now, I won't kill you. You know my reputation, so you know that I keep my word. I have no loyalty to Ernesto Alvarez; I only want the woman."

De Smet's gaze didn't waver, but Gavin could see the man was considering his options.

Killing Chloe meant the man lost all leverage. Giving her up might buy him some time.

"Mila violated her terms with Alvarez. His people are already on the way here. You need all the head start you can get."

Gavin kept his eyes on De Smet and lowered the gun. As fast as his vampire reflexes were, he didn't think he could shoot De Smet faster than the marksman could pull the trigger, so a firearm was useless. The marksman had seen Gavin use wind to knock his friend off-balance, so he had already braced himself. Gavin would have to convince him to let Chloe go.

"Leave now." Gavin put his hands up. "You haven't hurt her yet. I saw a door at the end of this hallway. Take your hands off my wife, leave now, and I won't kill you."

De Smet blinked. "Wife?"

Gavin cocked his head. "As I said, I have no loyalty to Alvarez. Take your hands off my wife. Leave now. I won't kill you. If you leave so much as a bruise, on the other hand..." He bared his fangs. "You won't like the result."

Gavin stepped away from the door, allowing De Smet to circle the room and move closer to the exit. He couldn't look at Chloe or he'd lose control and she could be hurt by the panicked human.

Once he was close enough to the door, De Smet moved with the fluidity of a trained soldier. He shoved Chloe toward Gavin, turned, and took two steps down the hall before Gavin heard a crunching sound, a slice, and a thunk as the gunman's head hit the ground.

Chloe turned and saw De Smet's lifeless eyes looking at her from the floor.

She turned to Gavin. "You said you wouldn't kill him."

"I didn't kill him." He took Chloe in his arms and enfolded her in a fierce embrace. "But I don't speak for Tenzin."

≈

CHLOE HAD NEVER BEEN WHOLLY comfortable flying with Gavin, but currently her boyfriend didn't trust the roads, cars, or anything but his own arms. So she kept her eyes forward, refused to look down, and trusted Gavin to keep her safe.

Safe.

She wrapped her arms around his neck and held on tight. Tenzin was in front of them, enclosing their party with a bubble of stillness so that Chloe felt nothing more than a slight breeze brushing against her legs as they crossed the midnight sky.

Ben was behind them; Chloe could see him over Gavin's shoulder. He kept watch, his startling grey eyes visible in the darkness.

"Almost to the Vecchios', dove."

Chloe nodded, but she said nothing. She was replaying the events of the night over and over in her mind, the endless questions, her frustration and panic trying to lead her two captors along with just enough information to keep them interested in a story she was making up on the fly.

She'd felt like Scheherazade, spinning tales on top of fantasies, inspired by nothing more than the desperation to survive. She's lost all sense of time between the four blank walls of her prison, so when she finally heard movement outside, everything seemed to happen at once.

The snake of a man in the corner struck. She'd never had anyone hold a gun to her head, but she immediately flashed back to the beatings she'd taken from her ex-boyfriend when she was young.

The fear was the same. The pain was less. The hard metal against her temple was startlingly similar to the handle of a golf club. She froze and slowed her breathing, trying to avoid any reaction that could make the unknown worse.

Gavin had exploded through the door, and in less than a second, the tall man who'd interrogated her was on the ground, his body a limp rag, and the gun she hadn't known he was carrying was in Gavin's hand.

"Is Zain okay?" Her voice sounded dull, even to her own ears.

"He was hit with a tranquilizer too. He'll be fine."

"I thought he was dead at first, but then when I woke up in that room, I was hoping he was alive. That maybe they didn't want to kill us." She felt her stomach drop as they started their descent. "They would have killed me."

"The vampire in charge of those men is dead. All her people will be dead before sunrise if they aren't already."

"I don't know if that makes me feel better or worse."

"The point is, no one is going to kill you. I'll explain more when we land."

The sky was cloudy when they dropped down suddenly, straight into the shadowed heights of the Vecchio estate.

In seconds, Beatrice had a blanket wrapped around Chloe. Giovanni was barking orders at everyone around them, and Gavin had his hand at the small of her back, shepherding her into the guesthouse where he had been staying.

The familiar scent of lavender and linen greeted her, and she smelled Gavin's cologne from a jacket hanging on the back of a chair.

A knot of fear began to unfurl in the center of her chest, and tears burned the back of her eyes.

"Chloe, what do you need?" Beatrice kept her voice soft. "There's water on the table, and I'm making tea. I already called your mother to tell her you're back, and Audra is explaining it to her as if it was all a misunderstanding—"

"Gavin." Chloe turned to him and allowed herself to fall apart.

"Everyone out!" Beatrice ordered.

Chloe clutched the front of his shirt and let the hours of fear and tension release, her body shaking as sweat bloomed over her body. "They were going to kill me. They thought I was someone else. They were going to kill me, but if I told them I wasn't Keisha, I thought they might try to kill her and I couldn't let that happen. I'm going to throw up."

"Beatrice!"

"I got it."

Someone shoved a trash can under her face, and Chloe heaved into it, nothing but a thin stream of acid leaving her. She hadn't been able to eat the day of her father's service. She'd had nothing in her stomach for nearly twenty-four hours.

"I'll get some water."

She closed her eyes and focused on the feeling of Gavin rubbing her back. "I told them what they wanted to hear—at least I think they believed me—but that horrible man Tenzin killed never stopped staring at me, and I knew he wanted to—"

"Breathe, dove." Gavin stroked her neck, her shoulders, her back. "Deep breaths."

Beatrice handed her a glass of ice-cold water, and she drank and drank until she felt the shakes begin to subside.

She took one deep breath after another. She knew she wasn't making any sense. She had no idea if Gavin even knew that the whole debacle had been a twisted kind of job interview.

"Keep breathing." He led her to the couch, sat down, and drew her into his lap, still rubbing her back. "I've got you, dove. The bad men are gone."

"You killed them," she blurted. "You killed them because of me."

"I did," he said quietly. "In my world, some things

cannot be negotiated. Threatening harm to a mate is unacceptable."

"But I'm not a vampire." She wiped tears from her cheeks and took the tissue that Beatrice handed her. "I'm not your mate."

"You are." Gavin's voice was rough.

"Gavin—"

"I know we're not married, Chloe. I know that."

Chloe saw Beatrice slip out of the room, leaving her and Gavin alone.

"But when they took you, I knew it was my fault. If they'd known what you are to me, they never would have dared. Mila would never have even touched—"

"Mila?" Chloe wiped her eyes. "Who's Mila?"

"She was the person I approached to form a new telecommunications business with before I went to Marie-Hélène. I decided not to collaborate with her because I didn't think she was trustworthy. Clearly I was correct. I never even imagined she would do something like this, however. Holding you as some kind of leverage—"

"That's not what they were doing though."

Gavin frowned. "Explain."

"Telecommunications?" Chloe nodded. "Like Nocht, you mean?"

"A Nocht competitor is what we're aiming for, yes. But with better hardware and more secure software."

She sighed. "Okay, everything makes a lot more sense now."

"What did they do to you, Chloe?" His hands were tight on her legs.

"Relax." She squeezed his hand. "There was no

torture or anything like that. They didn't use amnis. Believe it or not, they were trying to hire me."

He frowned. "For what?"

"This is the crazy part." She frowned. "They must have been following me, right? You said that happens sometimes because people want to know why you have so much security on a human employee."

"And most of them realize fairly quickly why you have security because we've never hidden our relationship."

"Exactly." They hadn't hidden it, but they hadn't publicized it either. Chloe was starting to see why that could be a problem. "They searched my name and apparently found a Dr. Reardon who works out of Boston in voice programming for robotics."

Gavin's eyes widened. "They thought you were your cousin Keisha?"

"How do you know—?"

"I met her and her fiancé at the reception the night before the funeral. Really, both of them are fascinating individuals. I only understood about half of what they were talking about, but they were clearly..." He caught her expression. "Sorry. They thought you were Keisha and that I'd hired you for the new company."

"They thought I had to be your ace in the hole or something, I guess."

His arms went around her, his amnis spread over her skin, and he hugged her to his chest, nearly crushing her. "You are, but not for business reasons."

Gavin's arms and amnis felt like a full-body embrace, and the pressure unlocked her body. Chloe's heart rate settled. The nausea subsided, and the painful tension in her back started to melt. She slid her arms around Gavin's abdomen and let herself relax, laying her head on his shoulder.

"They didn't hurt me," she repeated. "They didn't even threaten me. Not really." Though she had been completely terrified. "If they died because of me—"

"Chloe, a normal person—immortal or not—would not tranquilize an innocent man and kidnap someone from their mother's home in order to entice that person to work for them. That is unacceptable in any culture, mortal or immortal."

Chloe blinked. "I mean... Tenzin?"

"Tenzin is not normal, and I don't even think she would do something like this." Gavin's voice hardened. "If you had said no, do you think they would have let you go?"

No. Chloe had known that instinctively. It was why she'd tried so hard to stall. "I know what you're saying."

"Those men sealed their fates the moment they shot Zain, whether they realized it or not. He's Beatrice's driver, which means he's under her aegis, and her great-grandfather is the vampire regent of Southern California. Once Mila's people violated his trust and committed violence against one of his humans, Ernesto had no choice."

"Consequences."

"The rules in the immortal world are harsh, but they exist to keep a modicum of order within a community of calculating predators. Violence against humans who are under vampire protection must be avoided, or there will be chaos and vendettas would take over our world. Once Mila's men took that step, Ernesto had to act or his leadership would mean nothing."

"So... it wasn't really about me."

"For me, it was about you. But your captors signed their own death warrants the moment they took you and shot Zain." He squeezed her hand. "None of this was your fault."

11

Ben and Tenzin had decided to fly back to New York on their own, which meant that Audra, Semis, Gavin, and Chloe flew back three nights later on a private cargo plane, another of the customized fleet Gavin had invested in.

They'd taken a few nights to reassure everyone that Chloe was fine, her family didn't need to worry, and Gavin wasn't some gangster who had dragged the innocent Chloe Reardon into his dark and dangerous underworld.

Privately, Gavin thought that was a fairly accurate take. It didn't mean he was giving her up though. He also spent one of those nights introducing Chloe to Ernesto and the entire immortal court of Los Angeles as his mate. She'd been uncomfortable with that much attention on her, but Gavin convinced her it was a necessary evil.

Message sent. Territory claimed. It would take some time, but word would get around, and Chloe would be safer for it.

His lover settled into the plush beige seat of the

airplane and immediately reclined the seat. "I want to sleep for a week."

"Then you should do that." Gavin sat next to her and took out a print copy of the *Financial Times* he'd picked up in the private terminal in Burbank.

"Don't think I haven't forgotten that you called me your wife to that guy."

He glanced over. "I'm immortal, dove. That's more than enough time to convince you."

She didn't say anything, but she gave him a sleepy smile.

His internal monster sat up at attention, then settled down inside with a growling kind of satisfaction. Chloe hadn't run. He'd been terrified that she'd go back to her mother's house after her ordeal and decide that Gavin's life wasn't what she wanted, but it had been the complete opposite.

She'd started asking him about the phone calls he took. Acted curious about the plane-sharing scheme and how it worked. She eased him into questions about the vampire hierarchy of New Orleans and expressed excitement about moving to New Orleans while the new business was being started.

"Do you know that Louisiana is one of the few states in the country with no publicly funded dance companies? None." She frowned. "Can you imagine? It's both depressing and inspiring."

He looked up from a column analyzing the falling prospects of the ruble. Dance was far more interesting. "Inspiring how?"

"Well, obviously it's depressing that the state doesn't fund the arts, but that means that all the dance companies I'm finding online, all the studios and groups, they're all doing it purely out of love. That's *amazing*. To dedicate that much time to something because of passion?"

Gavin smiled and touched her chin. "Love can be quite surprising."

"Agreed." Chloe's smile turned into a slight scowl. "But it's also wrong—those dancers really ought to be paid." She looked back at her tablet as the plane started to move. "I've written down three groups that look interesting. Going to see if Phillip knows anyone in the area."

He touched a finger to her temple where he could still see the faint lines of a bruise from the barrel of Luc De Smet's gun. "Did you already tell Phillip you'll be moving for a while?"

"I told him six months, and he assured me he'll still have a place for me when I get back, so that feels good. I didn't tell him why we were going because..."

Because she hadn't known how to talk about his business before.

Gavin put his newspaper down. "If people ask what I do, tell them that in addition to a hospitality group, I'm also a venture capitalist. Most people don't really know what that means, but they'll accept a lot of moving around because of it."

She nodded. "That sounds about right."

"It's actually quite accurate." He picked up the paper again. "And of course, as my wife—"

"There's that word again."

He glanced over and saw the smile flirting around her lips.

Gavin leaned over, slid his hand around to cup the back of her neck, and kissed her, sinking into the sunshine scent of her perfume and the warmth she offered him.

What had he done to deserve her? Nothing. Not a damn thing.

"I'm the luckiest devil in the world," he muttered.

"You're sure a presumptuous one."

His lifted one eyebrow. "Am I?"

She smiled again. "Maybe."

He reached down and drew her right leg up and over his knees as the plane started to move. "I *am* the luckiest devil in the world." He patted her knee and turned back to the paper.

Instead of responding with the quip he expected, she was silent. He looked up and saw her staring into the distance as the plane took to the sky.

"What are you thinking about?"

"Did I tell you my father was thinking of going to my performance at Lincoln Center?"

"You did." She'd probably told him a dozen times. "I'm sorry he missed it, dove. You were brilliant." He squeezed her knee. "You always are."

She was looking at him. "You never miss my shows."

"There was the one you did for your friend Carrie that I missed because it was just the one night and I was in Spain."

She blinked, but the smile she offered him was brilliant. "You remember the single show you missed. One single show."

He frowned. "I don't understand."

"To everyone else, my father was the most honorable man they knew. Always thinking of his community, always giving to charity, always there to advocate for the disadvantaged." She looked out the window, staring at the starry night as they broke through the clouds. "And he *was* all those things. But for the people closest to him—my mother, me, his own family—he was kind of a stranger. He was cold and rigid. I could never be good enough for him, not even by performing at Lincoln Center." She took a deep breath and let it out slowly. "I was never good enough."

Gavin wanted to punch the dead man, but that wasn't possible or helpful. "You are more than enough, Chloe Reardon. You don't have to change the world to be enough."

The plane leveled off, and the low rumble of the engines melted into a dull white noise as the flight attendants began to prepare an evening meal for the human passengers.

Chloe looked back at Gavin. "To everyone else, you are a calculating, ruthless businessman. Never taking sides. Neutral to the point of being an opportunist."

He never took his eyes from hers. "And to you?"

"You're the man who never misses a show. The man who brings me tea in bed. The man who rubs my knee when it's sore and puts up with my mother's passive-aggressive insults. Plus you talked me through my trauma when I made the mistake of cutting bangs last year."

"The fringe really wasn't a bad look for you, dove. I will never understand why you reacted to it so violently."

She smiled, and he saw everything he'd ever wanted in her eyes. Love, yes. Respect. Acceptance. *Trust.* She'd seen the darkness, and she hadn't run away. She hadn't even blinked.

"My father was a man who had all the appearance of goodness but none of the heart. He wanted to impress the world, and he did."

He folded his newspaper and set it on the table. "I

don't give a fuck about the world's opinion; I only care about yours."

"I know." Her eyes watered up. "Don't you see? That means to you, I'm the whole world."

He swung the table back, lifted the armrest between them, and pulled Chloe into his arms. "Will ye marry me, Chloe Reardon? I promise I'll always bring you tea."

She turned and kissed him slowly. Then she smiled, and it was everything.

"Yes."

≈

Two months later...

CHLOE WATCHED Arthur's face bobbing on the small phone screen as he walked up Seventh Avenue in New York and she walked down First Street in New Orleans. Audra, still wary from Chloe's abduction in LA, walked beside her, keeping off camera so Arthur couldn't see her.

"So how is life in the Bayou City?" he asked. "Drew is threatening to come visit if you and Gavin don't come home soon."

"I would love to see you, but I highly advise not coming here in the summer." She'd caught the Saint Charles streetcar from her dance studio in Touro, so it was only a short walk home, but it was still summer and the sun was barely setting. "Do you see how much I'm sweating?"

His face got huge on the screen for a second. "Ew. Now I do. Yuck."

Audra laughed silently, and Chloe rolled her eyes.

"You look great too. Thanks."

"I mean, of course you look beautiful. Blah blah blah. Newly engaged woman happily in love with her hunk of a filthy-rich Scotsman and all that. Of course you look fierce and breathtaking. But... I'm just saying your hair is bigger than usual."

"Oh my God, it's so big, right?" Chloe shook her head and felt the mass of her curls swaying around her. "It's like, crazy big." She had yet to master a hair routine that would last through Southern Louisiana humidity. "I don't know what to do with it. I may end up just doing braids or something."

"Ignore me!" Arthur waved at someone off camera. "I like the hair, but also braids would be super fun. Everyone misses you. How's your mom?"

Chloe shrugged as she sidestepped orange cones marking torn-up brick walkways. "She seems okay. I was hoping with everything that happened, she might be a little more..."

"Not herself?"

"That's the thing, isn't it?" Chloe waited for a line of cars to pass on Coliseum. "We had next to no relationship before, and losing my father didn't bring about any great reconciliation. I'm not surprised, but I'm kind of disappointed, I guess."

Arthur stared at her through the camera.

"What?" Chloe asked.

"I just wish you were home right now. I can't be your pest of a best friend when you're so far away. Also, I cannot give you hugs and that's annoying."

She pressed her phone to her chest and kissed the screen. "Any better?"

"No. Ew. I love you, but you're so sweaty." Arthur waved at someone else. "Drew and I are going to his fancy friend's house in the Hamptons this weekend, and I am so grateful I didn't listen to all my bitchy friends who gave me shit about hooking up with a banker, because none of *their* husbands or wives have fancy friends with fancy houses in cool places by the beach, do they?"

"Gavin has a house in Bali, but I haven't been yet. Can you believe that? Bali."

"Fine! Your husband is way way way richer than mine—you don't have to rub it in."

She smiled. "We're only here for six months or so. But we are probably going to do the wedding down here because Gavin's aunt wants to host and she's all excited and since I don't like planning events, I just want her to do everything and I'll show up. As soon as we have a date in the fall, I'll tell you."

"I cannot believe I didn't know Gavin has a fabulous Black aunt in New Orleans who speaks French and runs the most amazing burlesque club in the Southern United States." Arthur looked like he was jumping up and down. "I mean, this explains so much."

"What does it explain?"

"Oh!" Arthur waved at someone else. "Okay, I'm at B&J and I have to go." He blew a kiss at the screen. "We need to talk about your dress next week because I'll murder you if anyone else designs it and no one wants that. Hi to Gavin and be good and I love you."

Arthur disappeared just as Chloe turned the corner onto Chestnut Street.

"So Arthur seems..." Audra waited at the gate. "Exactly like Arthur."

"Yep." She waved at Audra, who was living in a rented house a block away with Gavin's other security staff. "See you tomorrow."

"Let me know if anything changes; just text."

"Will do."

Chloe punched in an electronic code to open the wrought iron gate, using her hip to wedge the door open while she carried her workout bag and two sacks of groceries from the green market.

Gavin's property in New Orleans was surrounded by a high hedge that shielded the palatial house from prying eyes. It had a wraparound porch and two second-story balconies to accommodate the discriminating wind vampire.

The night air smelled of lilac and myrtle from the two enormous bushes that framed the kitchen door. A slow-moving draft followed her up the steps and into the kitchen door, teasing the back of her legs.

Chloe smiled; Gavin was awake and knew she was home.

She waved at the woman she met in the kitchen. "Hey, Miss Jackie. How are you tonight? I brought home some peppers and tomatoes like you asked."

"Thank you, honey. And I'm doin' just fine."

Jaqueline Dennely was Gavin's housekeeper in New Orleans. The older woman had to be in her fifties, but Chloe didn't know for sure. Her dark eyes held decades of wisdom, and her silver-and-black hair was pulled into an immaculate chignon, but her dark brown skin held not a single wrinkle. She was formal in an old-country way, always wore neatly pressed dresses, and kept the house polished to perfection.

Chloe had been worried the older woman wouldn't approve of her, but her immaculate appearance was only the exterior of a warm and generous soul. "Miss Jackie" had immediately made Chloe feel at home.

Jackie was chopping onions in a flower-dotted apron. "How was your practice today?"

"Really great. I think the director found a spot for us to perform next month."

"So soon?"

"Mm-hmm." She hung her workout bag in the laundry room off the kitchen. She'd once made the mistake of hanging it off the back of a kitchen chair and suffered a look from Jackie that made her feel about three years old.

"If you're headed upstairs" —the housekeeper pointed to a tray— "I have Mr. Wallace's tea ready."

Chloe saw the wooden tray with an insulated thermos of tea, two china cups, two small sandwiches, and a bunch of green grapes. "I'll bring it up; thank you."

"You're welcome. I'm putting together a chicken pilaf before I finish for the day. Message me if there's anything else Mr. Wallace needs."

She grabbed a grape and popped it in her mouth. "Miss Jackie?"

"Ye-es?"

Chloe asked, "Are you ever going to call Gavin by his first name like he keeps asking you to?"

Jackie sent her another *look*, this time with a raised eyebrow. "The real question is, will I be calling you Mrs. Wallace anytime soon?"

"You better not." She grabbed the tray and headed upstairs. "You know Marie-Hélène wants to make a giant party of this whole thing, so if you have any wedding questions, you better ask her, not me."

"You're the *bride*, Miss Chloe."

She laughed. "I am along for the ride. If you think I have any say in this business, you are very mistaken."

The kitchen flowed into the morning room and the family salon, which led to the formal dining room and the parlor and smoking room. Chloe ignored the fine furnishings that still felt like a museum and headed up the grand staircase in the entry hall.

The bedroom Gavin had set up was a variation on a European-style grand house with a husband's room and a wife's room on opposite sides of a shared dressing room, but in their case, it worked out perfectly since Gavin's room needed to be secured and light proofed while Chloe's did not.

She walked through her room to find Gavin sitting on the edge of her bed, watching the evening news on the television.

"Hey, handsome."

He was already dressed. Damn.

Gavin's smile was wicked. "Hello, my wife to be."

"Be serious with me." She poured him a cup of tea and added a little milk. "Is Jackie going to start calling me Mrs. Wallace after we're married?"

"Hmm." Gavin's eyebrows rose when he tasted the tea. "I do like the sound of that, Mrs. Wallace."

"You know I'm not planning to change my professional name. You told me it didn't matter to you."

"It does not, but if you think you're going to keep Jaqueline from calling you Mrs. Wallace, I wish you good luck. The woman has worked for me over thirty years and she still calls me by formal address." He shrugged. "She's old-fashioned."

"Speaking of old-fashioned, MHC's social secretary emailed me today with a prospective schedule for the wedding. It's five days, Gavin. Five days of events."

"And I am sure Marie will fill up every minute."

Gavin frowned and set his teacup down on her side table. "Have we even set a date yet?"

"No, but she says whatever we choose, it'll be fine because we'll have the whole event at her river house." Chloe held up her hands. "How many houses does she have?"

"Five that I know of," Gavin said. "Do you want to know how many we have?"

"Probably not."

"You'll find out soon enough," he muttered. "Come drink some of this tea."

She smoothed her hands over his crisp white shirt. "I don't want tea."

"Oh?" His hand slid from her hip, down her thigh, which was covered in soft blue leggings. "Whatever could you want, Mrs. Wallace?"

"I just got home from practice, so I'm all sweaty."

"Is that so?" His finger slipped under her waistband.

"And I was thinking I would take a shower and then..." She shifted to straddle his knee.

"And then?"

"You could give me... a massage." She smiled.

Gavin's hand slid back to cup her bottom. "Oh, dove, did you pull a muscle?"

"I might have." Her hands spread over his pressed shirt. "But then I came upstairs, and it looks like you're already dressed for work."

"You're right; I'm already dressed." He glanced down and slid his other hand between her thighs. "Of course, that's never stopped us before."

Chloe gasped. "Mr. Wallace, what would the house-keeper say?"

"She knows what kind of monster I am." Gavin pulled her closer. "Are you scared yet?"

"Not even close." Chloe leaned in and took his mouth in a decadent kiss. "I'm not afraid of the dark."

~

Find out what Gavin and Chloe are up to when they team up with
Brigid and Carwyn for an all new adventure in
PALADIN'S KISS,
coming August 2022 at all major retailers!

PREVIEW: PALADIN'S KISS

Brigid saw the flashing blue lights in the side mirror and her fangs dropped. She turned to her partner, who was driving the van. "I told you it was a speed trap."

Carwyn glanced to the side, then the rearview mirror. "I was barely over the limit." He started to pull over. "I'll do the talking, wife. You have a habit of rankling law enforcement."

Brigid glanced at the three unconscious humans in the back of their converted Volkswagen van and felt her fangs drop. "I can't imagine why."

The back of her throat burned when she smelled the human officers behind their vehicle.

"He's sitting on the hood of his car," Carwyn muttered. "No respect for the schedule of others."

"It's a tactic to make us nervous." Brigid rolled her eyes. "They definitely think we're carrying drugs."

"A Volkswagen camper van with California plates driving through rural Louisiana in the middle of the night?" Carwyn smiled as the man started to walk toward them. "I can't imagine why you'd think so."

She cranked down the van window and saw the outline of a second officer on the other side of the police cruiser, eyeing her window with interest in the blinding cruiser lights.

She spoke in Irish, unwilling to give any information to the humans. "There are two of them."

Carwyn glanced in the mirror. "Noted."

"If they search the car—"

"They won't." He was wearing a black button-down shirt dotted with bloodstains. He carefully buttoned it up to the neck.

Brigid frowned. "What are you doing?"

"Keeping us from having to incapacitate any more humans tonight."

She rolled her eyes and sat back, her eyes continuing to flick to the side mirror where it looked like the second officer had lit a cigarette.

Gimme.

Brigid stared at the glowing tip of the cigarette, the fire that lived under her skin pricking her to act; she pushed it back with practiced resolve.

Not tonight. Not here.

The human officer approached Carwyn's window, and the scent of his blood made Brigid's mouth water. She needed to feed, and not the blood in the drug-laced veins of the humans in the back of the van. This one smelled like he believed in clean living, mother's cooking, and wild game.

Delicious.

The police officer finally sauntered to the window. He was a human in his early forties if Brigid was guessing correctly. He looked tired and a little worn out.

Putting in the hours—Brigid recognized the expression. Punching the clock. This officer was sick of night shifts and bored to tears.

He cleared his throat and spoke in a broad Southern accent. "Evening, sir. Do you happen to know how fast you were going?"

It was if her husband turned to a pile of friendly Jell-O instead of the mountain of muscle he was. "Oh, I'm so sorry, Officer!" The Welsh vampire laid on a thick Irish accent.

Brigid snorted and covered her mouth, turning it into a cough.

He continued, "I do believe I was going eighty kilometers an hour, was I not?"

The officer frowned. "'Scuse me? Where y'all from?"

"Oh, surely we're from a humble Catholic mission in Ireland. I'm Father Cormac, and this is Sister Mary Clarence from the Sisterhood of the First Miracle in Kerry." He motioned toward her. "Sister Mary Clarence, wave hello to the nice guardaí." Carwyn turned to the officer. "She can't speak, sir, as she's recently taken a vow of *complete silence.*"

Jesus, Mary, Joseph and the wee donkey, she was going to kill him when this was over. Brigid leaned forward and waved.

The human frowned. "From... Did you say Ireland?"

"We're borrowing a vehicle from the parish in Los *Angeleez*, where we flew in from our last mission in..." He glanced at Brigid.

She smiled and pointed to her mouth.

"Fiji," Carwyn blurted. "We were on a mission to Fiji."

The police officer was already turned in circles from the accent. "I... I don't know where that is."

"Beautiful place." Carwyn nodded solemnly, his accent growing broader by the moment. "A beautiful part of the Lord's creation, full of heathen... cats."

She snorted again and covered it with a cough.

"Cats?" the officer asked.

"Yes, that's where we work, you see. In animal evangelism." A beatific smile spread over his face. "Working among the world's most vulnerable creatures to show the love of God to the voiceless." He nodded toward Brigid. "That's why my dear sister doesn't speak."

"Because of the cats?"

"Exactly. You don't eat the flesh of God's created animals, do you, young man? Ours is a strictly vegan mission."

The officer rallied. "Sir, can I see your driver's license? You were speeding."

"Was I? Surely not." Carwyn fumbled for his wallet. "The sign said fifty-five miles an hour there, and that's nearly ninety kilometers and I was doing only eighty."

The officer frowned. "Right. You were doing eighty in a fifty-five."

"But eighty is below ninety, so I don't see how I could be speeding."

Brigid could see the police officer doing the math in his head. "I don't... I'm not sure what you're used to—"

"I'm a law-abiding man, sir. A servant of God and the church."

Brigid's skin prickled when one of the humans in the back shifted his arm. The windows might have been curtained, but all the officer would have to do is look back and the three bruised and unconscious men would be visible.

Carwyn said, "We're trying to reach our new mission

in New Orleans, you see. There's a pack of feral dogs roaming the city that needs to hear the word of the Lord. Are you a Christian man, Officer?"

The man stammered. "Of course I am. I mean... I guess it's been a while—"

"Perhaps the Lord brought you to me and my dear Sister Mary Clarence tonight. Do you need to unburden your heart? Perhaps call your mother or grandmother? I have a mobile phone here and we can do that. Can I pray for you, Officer... I'm sorry, what is your name, sir? We could say a prayer right now. Together."

"Okay, just slow down." The police officer offered Carwyn a nervous laugh and patted the side of the vehicle. "There's your... blessing. Okay?" He stepped away. "Y'all keep it nice and below fifty-five and you'll make it to New Orleans safe and sound. Take the warning; keep it slow."

Go. Just go now. Brigid braced for another round of blarney from her mate. Carwyn had a tendency to push a bit too far, which more than once had caused more problems than it solved.

"Oh, bless you, young man." Carwyn made his voice creak just a little even though the officer looked older than the vampire did. "Bless you and your cats, sir."

"Right. Y'all have a good night and keep it slow."

Carwyn started the van and pulled into the road, leaving the still-flashing blue lights in the distance behind them.

"Can we turn back to the interstate now?" Brigid asked.

"As soon as we drop off our young friends here." Carwyn glanced across to her. "I see that you've chosen to break your vow of silence."

"Mary Clarence? We're making *Sister Act* jokes to the humans now?"

"Sister Mary Clarence had the voice of an angel; it was a compliment."

"Evangelizing feral cats in Fiji," she muttered. "I can't believe that worked."

"It wasn't the feral cats, darling girl. I threatened to call his mother and pray with him. I could see the Catholic guilt radiating as soon as I called myself Father Cormac."

"Never underestimate Catholic guilt." She saw a sign flash by. "Take the next right." She glanced at the human who'd moved before. "They're starting to wake up."

ALL VAMPIRES HAD an element given to them by their amnis, the immortal energy that lived within them like a current beneath their skin. Her husband was animated by the earth, the foundation of his energy, his immortality, and his massive strength. He stood over six feet with shoulders the size of a minor mountain range, a shock of red hair on his head, and a short beard he'd been growing for over a year.

So it came as no surprise to her that in addition to the handcuffs she'd used to secure the men to the railing, Carwyn had also buried them up to their waists in front of the sheriff's substation in Lafayette Parish.

They were definitely not wiggling out of that restraint.

In addition to the handcuffs, the men all had signs around their necks that advertised their crimes. One read: ASK ME ABOUT THE STOLEN PROPERTY IN MY GARAGE!

Another read: I STOLE THE BENSONS' CAR AND BEAT UP AN OLD MAN. And the last one had a sign that read: I DEAL DRUGS TO HIGH SCHOOL STUDENTS.

Carwyn clapped his hands together. "And that's what happens when you try to carjack a pair of vampires."

Brigid saw the moment the humans began to wake.

They were bruised and had to be aching, but she didn't have any sympathy. They'd attempted to disarm her husband with friendly banter and false welcome at their local pub before sticking a gun to his back in the hallway, forcing him to their van, and trying to rob them.

"Hello, boys." Brigid crouched down in front of the three men. "Remember what happened?"

What happened had been Brigid. The men didn't know that she'd followed them out and saw them pull the firearm. Unlike most vampires, Brigid knew what kind of damage a gun could cause on their kind if used in the right way.

No gun was going to end a vampire's life unless it completely severed the spine at the base of their neck, but a bullet wound anywhere along their nervous system could be catastrophic, if not life threatening. As best as Brigid could figure, amnis worked with the nervous system, so any serious damage to the spine or any major nerve could produce severe consequences.

She looked at the men. "You put a gun to my husband; that wasn't wise."

The ringleader of the group blinked slowly. "You have fangs."

"I do, but don't flatter yourself. I'd sooner drink from a sewer than your neck. I understand addiction—heroine was my candy—but that doesn't excuse the violence. Get help before you end up dead." She stuffed the number of a local rehab place in his pocket. "You don't want to meet me again."

He was still staring. "You have fangs."

"Jaysus." She stood and sighed. "What else should we do? Just leave them here?"

Carwyn was squinting at the darkness. "I think that's our only option. Do you think the alligators leave the bayou and go roaming?"

"Carwyn, if I have to deal with you chasing any more wildlife—"

"They wouldn't come and take a bite out of one of these two, would they?"

Brigid started to protest the men were fine, but she had to admit Carwyn might have a point. She crouched down in front of another one of the men. "Wake up." She patted his cheek, giving him a slight shock from her amnis when he was slow to come around.

"Fuck." The man jerked awake. "Where the hell am I?"

"How far can an alligator travel from water?" Brigid asked. "We're not from around here, so I don't know."

The man looked around himself in a panic. "George? Buddy?"

"Answer the question." She patted his cheek. "Alligators. Are you in danger from them if we leave you here?"

The man they called Buddy appeared to still be sleeping, but he spoke slowly and in an accent that Brigid barely understood.

"Yeah, gators gonna be a problem a'ight," he muttered quietly.

Did she care?

Not really, but Carwyn might.

Brigid stood and walked back to the van. "He said the alligators wouldn't be a problem."

Her husband frowned. "Are you sure?"

"Very sure. Come on now; we need to get to New Orleans before sunrise." She walked quickly to the van.

Carwyn started to follow her. "We'll call and report them from the highway."

"Excellent idea." That should get the men arrested before the creatures ate them.

The last thing Brigid needed was another black mark against her soul. Even if she was immortal, she'd face judgment eventually, and if she didn't, she'd have to face Carwyn.

They were heading back toward the highway within minutes, and Brigid sighed in relief. No more local police officers. No more shady characters at darkened petrol stations. They were back in the world of the American interstate system, replete with garish neon signs, brightly lit parking lots the size of football fields, and plastic-packaged food that smelled of chemicals.

"I need to feed," she said. "I was half hoping that police officer wouldn't fall for your friendly Irish priest bit and would cause us problems."

"We'll be at a safe club in two and a half hours. Can you make it that long?"

She cracked open a bottle of blood-wine and drank. "This should keep me from any road rage incidents."

"Good, but crawl in back to drink that unless you want another encounter with law enforcement."

She crawled in the back of the van and kicked her feet up on the bench. "Onward then."

"To the wedding!" Carwyn grinned as he took the on-ramp.

"To the wedding." Brigid took an extra gulp of blood-wine.

To the wedding.

The *wedding*.

On second thought, maybe she should have stayed behind with the alligators.

~

PALADIN'S KISS will be available at all major retailers in August 2022.

For more information, sign up for Elizabeth Hunter's newsletter or visit her blog at ElizabethHunterWrites.com.

AFTERWORD

Dear Readers,

It's here! The Secret Project is finally here!

I am so relieved. I am really horrible about keeping secrets, and when I decided to write another story for Gavin and Chloe, I knew I wanted to just bash it out, drop it, and loose it in the wild.

I needed fangs. I needed romance. I needed Gavin and Chloe!

(Plus, I wanted to get all of you excited about PALADIN's KISS in the fall.)

Who knows? Gavin and Chloe might even get me to write a wedding. If anyone could do it, it would be them.

I'm sure *all* of you are wondering if there will be another chapter to their tale, and I can confirm that yes, I am sure I will write more for them. I definitely envision at least one more story, but there could be more.

Remember though, at their hearts, these two wonderful characters are peace-lovers, and they try to avoid the spotlight as much as possible, unless it's to open a new club or a new dance program.

But do be ready for them to show up in this fall's PALADIN'S KISS, the third Elemental Covenant novel! I can't wait for you to read it.

Be well, and I hope you enjoyed THE DANCER AND THE DARK.

—EH

ABOUT THE AUTHOR

ELIZABETH HUNTER is a seven-time *USA Today* and international best-selling author of romance, contemporary fantasy, and paranormal mystery. Based in Central California and Addis Ababa, she travels extensively to write fantasy fiction exploring world mythologies, history, and the universal bonds of love, friendship, and family. She has published over forty works of fiction and sold over a million books worldwide. She is the author of the Glimmer Lake series, Love Stories on 7th and Main, the Elemental Legacy series, the Irin Chronicles, the Cambio Springs Mysteries, and other works of fiction.

ALSO BY ELIZABETH HUNTER

The Elemental Mysteries

A Hidden Fire

This Same Earth

The Force of Wind

A Fall of Water

The Stars Afire

The Elemental World

Building From Ashes

Waterlocked

Blood and Sand

The Bronze Blade

The Scarlet Deep

A Very Proper Monster

A Stone-Kissed Sea

Valley of the Shadow

The Elemental Legacy

Shadows and Gold

Imitation and Alchemy

Omens and Artifacts

Obsidian's Edge (anthology)

Midnight Labyrinth

Blood Apprentice

The Devil and the Dancer

Night's Reckoning

Dawn Caravan

The Bone Scroll

The Elemental Covenant

Saint's Passage

Martyr's Promise

The Dancer and the Dark

Paladin's Kiss

(August 2022)

The Irin Chronicles

The Scribe

The Singer

The Secret

The Staff and the Blade

The Silent

The Storm

The Seeker

Vista de Lirio

Double Vision

Mirror Obscure

Trouble Play

(October 2022)

Made in the USA
Columbia, SC
28 May 2022

61042513R00086